BLACK HEARTS AND RED TEETH

THE CONTINUATION OF A GIFT OF DEATH

DANIEL J. VOLPE

D & T
PUBLISHING

CONTENTS

1

A GIFT OF DEATH

THE AIR WAS full of teenage smells: cheap booze, weed smoke, nervous sweat, and cologne.

To Pat, these were smells of comfort, of his little kingdom of school.

The flames of the bonfire lit up the clearing in the woods. There was no official name for the spot, but high school kids had used it for generations to throw parties. It was far enough away the cops didn't bother with them, but close enough to town it wasn't an inconvenience.

Pat drank from a cup of beer. He was eyeing Tara, who was with a small group of girls on the other side of the fire. After the prank they played on Cameron, Pat and Tara began talking. It started innocently, just him trying his best to get her to send him legit nudes. She turned him down, but something about his asshole-ish charm drove her wild.

"You gonna hit that?" Tyler asked, walking up next to Pat, his beer in hand.

Pat looked at his buddy and smiled. "I didn't bring a tent and rubbers for nothing." He shook his friend's hand in a way that only douchebags do.

"My man," Tyler said. He took a sip from his beer. "Yeah, I'm hoping Marley will give me a blowjob later." He drank again. "She's on the rag, or else I'm pretty sure we'd be fucking. But I'll settle for a BJ."

"I hear she's pretty good." Pat sipped from his cup, hiding his smirk. He hadn't heard; he knew for a fact. Last week she blew him after school. Very random and very much appreciated.

"Holy shit!" someone said near the fire. "What the fuck are you doing here?"

Pat looked past his friend and into the crowd of other kids. They started huddling around someone, but Pat couldn't see.

"Let me through." Pat shouldered people out of the way, pushing through the crowd. After all, he was the king, and they were his subjects. He stopped and stood face to face with Cameron.

Pat laughed. "What the fuck are you doing here?"

It had been a week since Cameron's dick pic went viral. No one had seen him and the entire school thought he'd killed himself and was rotting in that shithole apartment.

"We thought—no, hoped—you'd killed yourself," Pat said, holding his arms wide, gesturing to the laughing crowd around him.

Tara stayed back, watching from a distance. Something moved in the dark woods behind her, but she couldn't see.

"Anyway," Pat said, stepping up chest to chest with Cameron, "this is a private party." He looked him up and down. "No cheese dicks allowed." The group laughed again, but some didn't. Cameron's calm was eerie.

Cameron smiled. "I'll be gone soon, but I have a gift for you." He started laughing.

Others laughed too, not out of humor but out of nervousness. The air felt heavy, pressing on them. It was as if a storm was getting ready to unleash.

"You don't have anything I could want," Pat said, his nose almost touching Cameron's.

"Oh, I don't know about that," Cameron said. "There," he pointed to Tara, standing by herself at the fire.

They all turned, staring at Tara. Then, not knowing what they were looking at, she turned around, peering into the gloom.

Sarin burst from the shadows. Her mouth was wide with razor-sharp teeth. Her clawed thumbs found Tara's soft eyeballs, plunging them deeply. The membrane burst, blood and ocular fluid running down Tara's cheeks. She roared in agony.

Sarin moved fast, locking her mouth over Tara's strained neck. She bit, releasing a spurt of gore, and ripped. Tara's throat was opened, a fan of blood spraying on the face of the vampire.

The crowd screamed and ran as Sarin dropped Tara's corpse and grabbed another girl by her ponytail. Sarin used her claws to pull her windpipe out before she bit her face off. Half of the girl's tongue lolled from the mangled meat. The vampire didn't seem concerned about feeding at the moment. No, she wanted to kill, and kill she did.

Pat stood frozen, watching the woman rip his friends apart. He'd forgotten about Cameron standing in front of him. He turned and looked into the dead, black eyes of the boy he so loved to torment. His bowels and bladder voided in a splash.

Cameron took in the fear-filled smell of piss and shit.

He smiled at his bully with a mouthful of fangs.

The sight of the elongated teeth shook Pat to his core. It was as if the carnage held him in place, but the view of the fangs released him. He tensed up, his brain telling him to fucking run. Finally, the urgent message reached his muscles, and he moved.

Cameron was fast. Much too fast for the human brain in Pat's skull, where it wouldn't reside for much longer. Cameron's clawed fingers sunk into the muscle of Pat's upper arm, down to the bone. The pulse of his severed brachial artery sprayed blood against Cameron's fingers. A delicate massage of gore.

Pat's face was pale, his color drained, and he looked like a boy made of chalk. The pain was numbing and intense at the same time. As if breaking your foot while it's asleep. He stared as blood seeped from his arm around Cameron's hellish fingers.

SCREAMS AND THE WET SLAPS OF EVISCERATION REPLACED THE SOUND of crickets and the night life. The *real* creatures of the night were out, and they were hungry for death.

Since his change and rebirth, Cameron's hunger was nearly insatiable. But, like a newborn child, an infant vampire needed to eat and he would eat.

The thick bundle of veins and arteries in Pat's neck throbbed. To the ordinary, naked eye, this would be a tiny blip—a minor tremor caused by fear and pain. But to a vampire, it was like a dinner bell ringing.

Before the attack, Cameron told himself he would make the boy suffer. To hurt him, humiliate him, laugh in his face as he ripped his guts out. But, faced with a pang of gnawing hunger, he knew that wasn't possible.

Cameron opened his jaws wide, further than he ever thought they'd be able to stretch. He could taste the bloody-mist in the air; it was divine. He brought his hell-born maw in closer, preparing to feed.

Pat was collapsing. He needed to be free and fast. His lips and tongue were dry. Despite the damage and fear, he had to escape.

"P-please," he croaked. "Let me go. I'm sorry."

Cameron paused. A drop of saliva fell on the boy's neck, and a tooth brushed against flesh, but he stopped. Then, slowly, processing what had been said, Cameron closed his mouth. It still felt odd, the elongation of his face to accommodate the mouth full of fangs, but he was getting used to it.

"Sorry?" he asked the bully.

Pat nodded. His sleeve was wet from the oozing blood. "Yes, truly I am." His tongue hissed against his dry lips as he tried to summon moisture.

A boy who was missing an arm, shambled by them and towards the darkness. The torn flesh and exposed bone looked like a war injury, not the victim of a vampire.

A flash of movement made Cameron's eyes shift as Sarin attacked the boy from behind.

Her hands, built for murder, grabbed the boy around the neck. She snapped backward and bit the top of his skull off. Sarin let the bone and brain fall from her mouth and his corpse hit the ground in a heap. Then, in a flash, she was off again—the perfect killing machine.

Killing.

Feeding.

Cameron had work to do. As much as he wanted to watch Sarin and her dance of death, he was hungry. Oh, so hungry.

Pat was crying. His body resorted to the last options of defense: weep and beg and when that doesn't work, weep and beg more.

Cameron plunged his free hand into Pat's gut, just under his ribcage. The liquid sound of entrails severing was loud in his ears, like a symphony of death. He didn't take his eyes off the boy's face and relished his pain and fear.

Pat wriggled, almost seized against the violation occurring in his body. Instead, he burped blood into Cameron's face; the rest drooling down his chin.

Cameron licked the droplets with his long tongue, savoring the taste. His fingers burrowed, slashing open organs in their quest. Then, they found their mark.

Pat's heart felt like a caged bird under Cameron's hand. It was in code red and firing on all cylinders. The powerful muscle did everything it could to keep the body alive, but the struggle was fruitless.

Cameron stroked the beating heart, knowing it wouldn't beat for very long. His claws dug small furrows in the meat, and his fingers wrapped lovingly around it. He yanked.

A fan of blood sprayed onto Cameron's smiling face. Pat's pain mask was a thing of beauty. Pure art.

Cameron's arm slithered out of the boy's chest cavity, which would only be a few seconds longer in agony. His hand was slick with gore, bile and stomach matter, and clenched in a wicked fist, was Pat's heart. Cameron raised the dripping and quivering organ to his face. He breathed in the aroma of hot blood—the iron smell, the basting of adrenaline, the fear—it was all delectable.

Life was fading from Pat's eyes, but Cameron hoped there was enough left. Just a moment of clarity left in the boy's brain to witness his gory meal.

Cameron opened his mouth again and bit the heart like an apple. His fangs made quick work of the muscle. A torrent of meaty ichor flooded his senses, nearly overwhelming him. He'd fed before, but this meal, this was special. In another bite, he finished the heart.

Pat was dead, but a few partygoers were still alive, albeit badly wounded. Cameron dropped Pat's body and hunted.

Tyler lay on the forest floor. His hands struggled to contain the wriggling loops of purplish red guts that danced through his fingers. He writhed and moaned, not caring what beast he attracted. The injuries were jagged and numerous. Sarin must've cut him down while moving to kill another.

Cameron stood over the wounded boy. He turned his head like a dog, hearing a whistle in the distance.

"No..." Tyler began, but his face scrunched in agony, "don't." His muscles flexed and spasmed from the pain. His hand clenched, and a finger pierced his intestine. A thick slurry of feces pushed from the wound like an overstuffed sausage.

Cameron's stomach growled. The heart was delicious, but he needed more. He required the hot release of an open artery, gushing blood into his throat. The urge was insatiable—he needed it right away. Cameron fell upon the boy, his mouth open wide. Sharp fangs pierced both sides of Tyler's neck. The boy's pulse was like a fire hose waiting to be punctured. Cameron's fangs did just that, ripping through flesh. His mouth was instantly full of blood. The taste and sensation were nearly orgasmic, and each gulp unleashed more and more. He bit harder, willing the dead flesh to give to him, to satiate his bloodlust, but the supply had run dry. Cameron's eyes, tuned for the night, scanned. A girl, one who he didn't recognize, lay on her back. Her eyes were open, and her chest rose, but she didn't move.

Paralyzed, he thought, a grin split his wicked face as he sauntered over.

"Hello," he said, looking down at her.

A tear. One solitary tear slid down her cheek.

THE NIGHT WAS QUIET AGAIN, BUT NOT SILENT. THE FIRE CRACKLED and bugs chirped. But another sound ruled the night—the sound of vampires feeding.

DULL EMBERS, SNAKES OF BLACK AND RED, DANCED IN THE FIRE PIT. There was no more light from the coals, but Cameron and Sarin didn't need it.

The vampires lay on their backs, looking at the stars through the branches. It was a clear night and even in the woods, the full moon —a predator's moon—shed its silvery light.

The scene around the fire ring was one of chaos. Bodies, offal, limbs, skin, and blood puddles littered the forest—trees decorated with discarded organs thrown by enraged vampires. A severed head, torn from the top jaw and up, was covered in leaves and dirt. Nude flesh lay pale, even more so in the moonlight. A nipple from a ruined torso was the only dark mark on that chunk of meat. Mouths were locked in screams, screams that no one would ever hear. Underwear lay soiled—the last act of humiliation before death.

To Sarin and Cameron, it was art. It was beauty. It was who they were.

Children of the night.

Fearful of the sun.

Immortal killers.

Considerate lovers.

Vampires.

"Do you feel better?" Sarin asked. She used a girl's buttocks as a pillow, keeping her head out of the dirt.

Cameron took a breath, something he didn't think he'd ever do again after the night with the vampire hunters. His black heart fluttered; his stomach full.

"Yes, much better," he turned on his side, looking at Sarin in the moonlight.

She was beautiful and terrifying, like a great white shark moving through the sea's murky depths. Not nearly as scary as she had been a few weeks prior, but she still demanded respect. Her skin was porcelain white and her lips were full. She was stunning even when she was 'changed' into her vampiric form, like a king cobra with its hood spread. She would hypnotize you, make you lose yourself in her teeth and black eyes until you would practically give anything to be her meal.

Sarin turned and looked at him. Her black hair fell across her face, and she brushed it back behind her ear. They were close. Close enough to see the redness on the other's teeth. Close enough to smell the blood on their breath.

"So am I," she said, a smile playing over her lips. "They had it coming anyway." She patted the corpse of the girl she was using as a pillow. "Plus, they were delicious."

Cameron laughed but didn't mean to. They were delicious, that was for sure, but he didn't quite know how that made him feel. Was he wrong for what he was? Was he a monster for wanting death and human blood? No, he didn't feel like it. If he was a monster, then his mother was the devil that abused him. That made him live in squalor. Who would whore herself out for alcohol and steal from him. No, he was just fine.

Sarin propped herself up on an elbow. Her tank top was pulled down just a little but was more than enough to expose extra cleavage, of which she had an ample amount.

"Do you know what I like to do after feeding?" she asked, running her blood-caked fingers through Cameron's beard.

Cameron felt like prey under her piercing eyes and could feel himself stiffening. He gulped, remembering he was still an 18-year-old virgin.

"Ah," he stammered and licked his lips. He wanted to say *fuck*, but his brain wasn't working. A beautiful, no, gorgeous woman was touching him, touching and looking at him in a way he'd never seen before. "No?" he stammered.

Sarin smiled at him, her perfectly human teeth glowing white. "Oh, I think you do." She leaned in and kissed him.

Their tongues met in a wave of bloody spit.

Even though they were immortal, Sarin clearly didn't want to waste time. Her hand ran down Cameron's stomach, finding his erection straining against his pants. Then, expertly, she undid the zipper and snap, releasing his cock into the night air.

Cameron shuddered at her touch. He could feel her urgency, the hunger in her kissing. It was animalistic, and she nipped his bottom lip.

"Get these fucking things off," she demanded before plunging back into his mouth.

Cameron had never wanted to remove his pants worse than he did at that moment. He pushed at them, the dirt rubbing his exposed skin, all while maintaining the deep kiss. His pants weren't off all the way, but more than enough.

Sarin ripped her lips from his, almost as if annoyed, and began shedding her clothes.

Cameron gazed at her in awe. Her breasts hung just a little but were full. The coolness of the night air had her nipples puckered and stiff, and he wanted them in his mouth in the worst way. Her vagina was smooth, with just a thin patch of black pubic hair leading to her glistening slit. He swallowed hard, tasting her spit in his mouth.

Sarin stood, preparing to mount him. Then, slowly, she lowered herself down.

"I-ah," Cameron started and stopped.

Sarin was in mid-squat, hovering above his erection, which lay on his belly. A growing drop of pre-cum wet his shirt.

"What?" she asked. She lowered herself down, sitting on his thighs. Sarin took his cock in her hand and caressed its helmet, using his juices as lube. She heard him shudder and looked at his face.

Cameron was holding back. His eyes were closed, and he was panting.

Finally, it hit her. "Are you a virgin?"

He opened his eyes, trying to maintain his composure. Embarrassed, he said, "Yes, technically."

Sarin smiled and leaned down. Her breasts pressed against his chest, and she let her hair hang next to his face. Their noses touched, and she breathed him in, still holding onto his manhood.

"Oh, don't you worry. I'll take care of everything." Sarin pecked him on the nose and rocked forward, guiding him into her.

Cameron gasped. The stars seemed brighter than ever.

THE NIGHT WAS ALIVE. THE KIDS FROM THE PARTY...NOT SO MUCH.

Sarin and Cameron lay nude, piles of discarded and bloody clothes making up their bedding.

Cameron's black heart beat slowly and he never felt more alive. Sarin was right; she had taken care of everything. It was a wild, snarling and fast encounter, but it was one he'd never forget. One he'd never want to forget. If, a few weeks prior, someone had told him he'd lose his virginity to a gorgeous, older woman, he would've laughed in their faces. If they had told him not only was she smoking hot but also a vampire, he would've had them committed.

Cameron looked at the stars through the branches. It was a clear night, but he knew he saw more than ever. As if seeing life for the first time. The first time he felt free. All it took was death to give him the life he wanted. But what was this life destined to be? Chasing teenagers in the woods? Feeding on the blood of people, filling his vampiric lust for gore? And, better yet, what about him and Sarin? He wasn't stupid enough to think they would spend eternity together. What else was there? Would she raise him, like a mother and child, finally releasing him into the world on his own to hunt and kill?

He thought back to the two men at the camper, sent to kill Sarin and Vee-Exx. He didn't get to speak with Sarin much after his transformation, but she told him about those men.

They were vampire hunters—God honest vampire hunters who hailed from an old family.

After he was turned and had his wits about him, Cameron couldn't believe his ears. The fact vampires *actually* existed, and that there were families of vampire hunters, was almost too much for him to take in. If they existed, there had to be more. He didn't know if he could survive alone, especially against trained killers. Against scared and unsuspecting humans, there was no issue. He was a shark in a school of minnows with his new powers. Killing his former classmates had been exhilarating, but he felt slow and clumsy next to Sarin, a real death-dealer. Watching her in action was like watching a ballet of murder. The way she moved, her effortless kills and no-mercy wounds. It was all perfect. Years of practice, generations of bloodletting and death. Calculation. That was the best word for it. Each swipe of her hellish claws or bite from her jagged maw was brutally calculated.

Cameron had many questions, but one was nagging him more than others. Finally, he turned and looked at the nude goddess lying next to him.

The moonlight made her glow silver. Sarin's black hair was fanned out around her head like an evil crown. Her lips were full and just slightly parted. She stared at the sky, not blinking, and gently slid her tongue over her human teeth. Her hands rested over her breasts, not out of modesty but comfort.

Cameron had a difficult time finding the words. Even though they were locked together, biting and fucking, just moments earlier, he was in awe of her. He rubbed his beard and looked past her into the night, the question hanging on his lips.

"Something on your mind, lover-boy?" Sarin, sensing his angst, turned towards him. She adjusted the shredded hoodie she used as a pillow and faced him. Her hands fell away, revealing her breasts again.

Cameron hard-swallowed, tasting blood and her saliva. He fought to keep eye contact, but it was a losing battle. He stared and adjusted, hoping to keep his gaze on her face and not her chest.

Sarin smiled. "You can look, but remember, you have an eternity to look." She reached out and touched his face. Her nails were dark with dried gore and dirt.

Cameron shuddered and didn't think his cock would ever be soft again.

"I-I just wanted to ask you something." He looked away from her, trying to form the question in his brain.

"Anything." She scratched at his beard. The hiss of her nails through his hair was pure seduction.

"How—ah—how long have you—have you..." he trailed off, hoping she understood his childish and stammering question.

"Been a vampire?" She finished for him and cupped his chin, drawing his eyes to hers, giving them nowhere to go.

Cameron nodded slightly.

"It's okay to say it." She opened her eyes even wider, ensuring he was paying attention.

There was nowhere else Cameron's attention could've been at that moment or any other moment for the rest of his life.

"We're vampires, Cameron. Blood-hungry, immortal killers who feed on death and murder. We are perfect predators and that is what we are. That is what *you* are. So, don't be ashamed. A fox doesn't apologize to the rabbit or the hawk to the mouse, right?"

Cameron smirked. "No. You're right."

Sarin blew him a kiss. "Of course, I'm right." She furrowed her brows. "What was the question again?"

"How long?"

Sarin smiled at him. "Do you remember the Civil War?"

"Ah, yeah. We learned about that in school. It was a major topic this year."

"Well, I *actually* remember it," she said with a smile.

Cameron's mouth didn't quite hang open, but he was shocked. It didn't seem real.

"Wow," he muttered. And before he could even think about it, he asked, "Who created you?"

Sarin's eyes shifted. They didn't go dark, which would've been nearly impossible with how black they already were, but they changed. Harder. That's what they became—guarded, as if Cameron had struck a sore spot.

Slowly, her hand fell away from his face. It wasn't a quick pull or done out of spite, but out of concentration. Then it was her turn to stare past him into the night.

After a moment, Cameron spoke, telling her he was sorry if he overstepped, but Sarin beat him to it.

"His name was Marcellus Baciu. He was my creator. He saved my life...more than once."

She didn't speak again, instead staring off.

Cameron watched her. A pang of jealousy stung him. But, of course, he had no reason to be jealous; this Marcellus guy was probably long gone and dead. And even if he was alive, Sarin wasn't trying too hard to find him. Nor him for her.

The silence between them seemed to drag out for eternity. A pop from the smoldering embers released a small shower of sparks into the night air.

Cameron spoke. "Well..." he drew it out, hoping she'd give him more info.

Sarin's eyes left the ether and returned to his, but she didn't speak, just shrugged.

"What happened with you and this Marcellus guy?"

Sarin smiled and mocked. "*This Marcellus guy?* I don't think you'd be referring to him like that if he were here. Marcellus is— was," no one knew if he was dead, but there were rumors he was killed in the 1970s, "one of the oldest vampires I'd ever met in my entire life." She was coming alive with memories, the emotions playing on her delicate face and porcelain skin. Sarin adjusted, leaning on her elbow. "When I met him, he was pushing 225 years."

Cameron wasn't the best in math, but knowing how old Sarin was, he knew Marcellus was damn near ancient.

"And, he wasn't even the oldest one. At least in the world. In the States, yes, he was among the oldest and strongest. A true fucking killer, but he could glamor anyone. They elected him Mayor in a small town once." She laughed at the memory. A life lost and gone.

"Really?" Cameron asked, feeling like he was being put on. The fact he was a vampire and had just slaughtered a classroom worth of kids made anything possible.

Sarin nodded. "Yes, he was something alright." The look of longing appeared again, but she brought it back to the present. "He could do whatever he wanted and most of the time did."

The jealousy, which had never left, was burning. Cameron had just lost his virginity to this 'woman,' and now they were reliving her past with another man. Albeit, this 'man' was an almost 500-year-old vampire who hadn't been seen for nearly fifty years. Nevertheless, his teenage heart, as black as it now was, trembled with jealousy.

"Oh, he sounds great," Cameron remarked.

Sarin smiled. Not just from stories of her first love and creator, but from how much of a human Cameron still was.

"Oh, he was great, that's for sure. A little too great and well...."

Cameron knew she was baiting him. Almost as bad as the dick pic, which landed him in his current predicament. But, girls, he was finding out, were his weakness.

"If he was so good, why'd you two separate?"

Sarin was waiting for that question. She'd often asked this herself, but it wasn't one she would answer. Instead, she slid closer to him, her hand landing on his chest.

"Let's save that for another time, shall we?" Her fingers traced the path of hair on his stomach and continued south.

Cameron might have a jealous streak, but he was still in an 18-

year-old body. His cock twitched, almost begging her to grab it. He was hard, harder than he was earlier.

"I think we can drop it…for now," he smiled at her. He gasped as her icy hand wrapped around his slick cock.

"Sounds like a plan to me," she leaned in and kissed him. Sarin knelt to get back on top.

Cameron put his hands on her shoulders and broke the kiss. "No," he said, staring into her gorgeous face. "I think I can figure it out."

Sarin squeezed his cock one last time before releasing it. "Oh, really?" she grinned but was already breaking away from him.

"Really." Cameron was sitting up.

"Well." Sarin gathered a pile of bloody clothes, making a pillow. Her elbows rested in the dirt and she thrust her ass into the air.

Cameron stared. Her vagina, glistening in the moonlight with wetness, was the most beautiful thing he'd ever seen.

"Have at it," Sarin cooed, putting her face against the sticky wetness of blood.

Cameron positioned himself and took a deep breath. "Don't mind if I do."

2

PILES OF ASH

JOHN TOSSED the crust of his toast onto the plate. His appetite had been little since losing his son, Nathan, but the last few weeks had been an absolute nightmare. He pushed the plate away, knowing that half a piece of toast was the only thing he'd eat until Marne came back to cook his dinner. Then, as if she could read his thoughts, Marne walked into the large dining room.

"Are you finished, Mr. Calderon?" Marne asked, looking at the half-eaten breakfast.

John didn't speak right away, but not out of rudeness. At least intentional rudeness. No, he was scanning the news on his laptop for anything that would help him.

"Perhaps I can make you something else?" Marne asked, standing at his side, awaiting an answer. It was getting late in the morning, and she needed to bring her son to school.

"Oh, sorry, Marne," John said, pulling his attention from the screen. "I was just, ah, trying to find something." He took his glasses off and rubbed his face. He was tired, bordering on the verge of exhaustion. John was not a spring chicken and his fifties had been kicking his ass, but still, he was more tired than he had the right to be. He'd read before that stress was a major killer in men, and John had more anxiety to last five lifetimes. "No, I'm fine. Thank you." He flashed her a strained smile and pushed the plate towards her.

"Okay," she took it and paused. "I'm sorry if this is over the line, but you need to eat."

John smiled. It was genuine and even reached his baggy eyes. He liked Marne, he did. Since the death of Nathan, things had been terrible. His wife was gone, a part of his life he'd like to erase, except that she gave him his son. His friends at the firm were shallow and, honestly, only just put up with him. And that was on thin ice. Not that it mattered. After the fucking vampires killed his son, he'd become obsessed. Obsessed with killing them, with ridding the earth of the killers they were. Obsessed with destroying them and any who'd help them. Obsessed with vengeance.

"I know," he said. "I'm just not feeling great this morning." He picked up his cup of black coffee and sipped. John drank a lot of coffee. He felt it running through his veins; it was the only thing that kept him awake. When he wanted to sleep, he'd smoke a joint, something he used to do as a kid. When Nathan disappeared, the nightmares invaded his brain. Sleeping pills didn't help either. They'd knock him right out but didn't shut down his thoughts. They made his nightmares even worse. The marijuana was his savior for restful sleep or relaxation. He smoked it more and more, which he didn't mind—anything to calm his brain, which was far from relaxed at the moment.

Marne stood with the plate in her hands and a motherly look of disdain. Even though she was young enough to be his daughter, she was still a mother.

"Okay, well, maybe you'll feel up to eating dinner." She checked her phone for the time and knew she'd be cutting it close. "Do you need me for anything else? The house is clean, and I'll fold the laundry tonight, but you'll have clean clothes in the dryer in twenty minutes."

John put his glasses back on and turned his attention to the computer.

"No, I'm good. Thank you, Marne," he said, with eyes glued to the screen.

She turned and walked away, shutting the door on her way out.

John closed the browser and opened another file that seemed to grow by the day. His cursor hovered over the icon, and John realized he was wheezing. He clicked and scrolled.

Pages and pages of records on the vampires. Hundreds of articles about mysterious disappearances and gruesome deaths. There was a file full of crime-scene photos, which had taken some sweet talking and generous donations to obtain. John scrolled to the bottom of one of the newest articles and opened it.

THE LOCAL: YOUR NEIGHBORHOOD NEWS

MAY 16TH, 2019

BY: LUCAS MANGUM

THE POLICE ARE STILL TRYING TO FIGURE OUT WHAT HAPPENED ON THE night of May 14th, but at this time, there are no leads in the gruesome scene. A local man, hiking through the Neversink Nature preserve, stumbled upon a world of chaos. The charred frame of a camper still smoldered, drawing the man in. Upon closer inspection, the man discovered numerous corpses. The police were contacted immediately and arrived on the scene.

Detective McLaughlin, the lead detective on this case, made the following statement:

"ON THE MORNING OF MAY 15TH, A CONCERNED CITIZEN CALLED 911 TO report a fire with casualties. Members of the Elk Park PD were dispatched to the scene. Upon officers arrival, they discovered a smoldering 2003

Coachmen camper. The camper appeared to be unoccupied, but an unknown pile of ash was discovered and is being sent to forensics for examination. In the vicinity of the camper, three corpses were discovered. The deceased, whose names are being withheld at this time, were all males, ages 28, 33 and 32. There are no motives at this time, but it appears to have been a botched robbery. Other leads are being followed."

The Elk Park PD has not commented further, and we'll keep you advised of any updates on this case.

John read it over and over. Since the day of the article, the names of the dead men were released. He didn't care about the third, but the other two concerned him. Cyril and Nestorius Visser. He wasn't worried about being linked to the two dead men; he was too bright. What did bother him was the fact the job hadn't been completed. One of the vampires might have died, burned alive in the camper, but at least one of them escaped.

John closed the file and pulled up the browser. He opened the news clip. The one he couldn't bear watching again, yet he forced his eyes to do it.

TEENS SLAUGHTERED, the headline read. John clicked on the 'play' button over the video.

"I'm Sandra Sanderson, reporting live from the scene of a horrific event. An event that's rocked the small town of Brighton, here in suburban New York." Sandra was in the woods, shedding her typical flashy dress for a more practical pair of jeans and a tight sweater. Behind her was a line of police tape and a bunch of impromptu walls made of PVC piping and blue tarps. "As you can see behind me," she gestured to the crime scene, "the scene is still very active and large." Uniformed police and plain-clothes detectives were scouring the woods. The occasional Tyvek-suited crime scene investigator would pop out from behind the tarped-off area. However, none would comment, and she'd stopped trying. "The police are still searching for clues as to what happened to these children, but an undisclosed source has stated, and I quote, 'This is a massacre like nothing I've ever seen before. Bodies everywhere, torn apart. It looks like someone got these kids with a woodchipper,' end quote." Sandra tried to look solemn, but she was the first news reporter on the scene and knew this story could make her career. Maybe even landing her behind the anchor desk one day soon. She tried her best to whip up some fake tears for the camera but couldn't. She wasn't that good of an actress. "The police urge residents to stay out of the area as they investigate this horrific scene. Some experts believe it may be a pack of wolves that migrated from upstate New York or possibly Canada. Others are calling that practically impossible. Only time and a thorough investigation will tell. Stay tuned for mor—"

John had seen enough. He closed the video and sighed.

More death. More grief. More tears shed by parents who'd never know what *truly* happened to their children. At least they'd get to bury them…what was left of them. It wasn't fair that beasts like vampires roamed the earth. They were an abomination, an affront to God, or whatever ruled the universe. They were a menace that had to be stopped. John had tried and failed. His haste to have them killed led him to hire sub-par vampire hunters. Not only was the job not completed, but more blood was spilled. He dragged two brothers into his mess and got them slaughtered, left for dead in the woods.

John sipped at his cold coffee, staring blankly at the wall. He wasn't done, no, not by a long shot. He'd kill all of them, but this time he'd be smart about it. He wouldn't hire amateurs or someone with a lineage of killing. He'd get true, tested killers, hunters of the undead.

It would take time and money, but there was no price too high. Even if it killed him, he'd see the vampires as piles of ash.

3

THE BLACK HEART

TWO YEARS later

REGGIE COULD FEEL THE PULSE OF THE SPEAKERS WHEN HE PULLED UP
outside the nightclub. It wasn't offensive or even loud, but the
steady thrum of subwoofers was like a heartbeat. He could feel the
energy pumping from the building, like it was alive.

"Are you guys kidding me?" he said, turning to his group of
friends in his car. "Are we seriously going to this place? Of all the
great clubs in the city, and we're going to the fucking Black Heart?"

Reggie pulled down his glasses, which were only clear glass and
not prescription, to make a point. Then, he looked at each of his
friends, waiting for their response.

Sitting in the back seat next to Luke, Mandy looked at him and
pouted.

"Oh, come on," she whined. "This place isn't bad. The music is,"
she searched for the right word, "decent." The other two passengers
grumbled mild approval. "But, the drinks are cheap and strong, plus
there's no cover."

"Yeah, man, there aren't many places you can get shitfaced for less than fifty bucks. Besides, there's usually some skanky goth girls here, so that's a plus," Luke said, not wanting to look at Mandy.

"Oh, is that what we're here for?" she asked, staring at him. Mandy knew he was joking, but she was never sure after his 'accidental blowjob' with a slut from school.

Luke flashed her a grin. "Come on, babe, you know I love you." He slid closer and put his arm around her bare shoulders. With his right arm draped over her, he put his left hand on her knee. Gently, he began working it up her thigh. "Do you know what I'm gonna do to this pussy later?" he whispered, his lips almost brushing her ear.

"Ahem," Lorrie said from the front seat. She looked back at her two friends, who needed to be stopped before they started fucking in the car. "Can we get inside and get drunk, please?"

Luke pulled his hand off Mandy's thigh and let her go.

"Yes, mom. No fun for us," Luke said and paused. "Oh, shit, speaking of fun." He sat up to get easier access to the pockets of his skinny jeans. "I grabbed a few of these bad boys today." Luke pulled out a small bag with pink pills in it. "Ladies, gentlemen," he looked at Reggie and smiled, "and Reggie, would you like to start tonight the right way?"

Lorrie's eyebrows went up. "Is that E?" she asked, leaning forward to look at the non-descript little pills.

Luke smiled at her and turned to Mandy. "Yup, I scored them today. I figured that even if this place is shit tonight, we won't care." He opened the bag and pulled one out. He tossed it in his mouth and grabbed his Kombucha to wash it down. "Ah," he said, smacking his lips together. "Gotta take your vitamins, boys and girls." He offered the bag around. "Anyone else?"

"Fuck yes," Lorrie said, grabbing the bag from him. She tossed one into her mouth and dry swallowed it. "You?" she asked Reggie, holding the bag.

Reggie looked at the pills and almost reached out, but stopped. He wanted one, especially hearing how *frisky* Lorrie was when on them, but he couldn't. He was the designated driver for the night. It was his turn and of all nights, it was the night when Luke had some primo drugs. He knew the drugs were essential if he ever had a chance to get in Lorrie's pants finally.

"Nah, I have to drive you fools, remember?" he said, putting his hand up to deny the pills.

"Suit yourself," Lorrie said, giving him an almost disappointed look. "I guess the three of us will have some fun." She handed the bag to Mandy, who gobbled a pill.

"I can't wait." Mandy took a sip of Luke's nasty drink and washed the pill down. She then handed the bag back.

Luke sat up again, pocketing the remaining pills, a shit-eating grin on his face.

"Don't worry, Reg, I'll take care of both of them." He winked at his friend.

"Excuse me?" Mandy asked. She was checking her make-up on the front-facing camera on her cell phone. She pulled the screen away from her face and looked at Luke. "I'd better be the only one you're taking care of tonight."

Luke smiled that douchebag smile. He'd be fucking Mandy later, but everyone had heard things about Lorrie. If he could be alone with the two of them, high on Ecstasy….

"Ow, what'd you hit me for?" Luke yelped, snapping out of his threesome daydream. He could see the playful scowl on Mandy's face.

Luke slid close, pressing against her so his face was in the camera's frame.

"Knock it off, would ya," he said, putting his cheek against hers. "Let's take a selfie and head in."

Mandy smiled a wry, horny little grin and tilted her head. The flash was blinding, but the picture was postable for the Gram.

"Fun night out. Getting twisted with my boo," she said as she typed out the caption for the photo before posting it online. "And… there, now we can start the night."

"Great, about fucking time," Lorrie said. She turned to Reggie. "Let us out and go park this thing. We'll meet you inside." She was already opening the door as if he didn't even have a say in the matter.

"Great idea, Lor," Luke said. He opened his door. "I will escort you ladies in, safe and sound."

"See you in there," Mandy said, before joining the other two in the cool night air.

Reggie watched them walk away, and the stab of jealousy stung just a bit.

Luke put his arms around both of their waists, but his right hand wandered to Mandy's ass, squeezing it. Then, slowly, as if by accident, his left drifted to Lorrie's firm backside. She didn't push it away.

"Motherfucker," Reggie said to no one. He put the car in drive and looked for a spot.

THE BLACK HEART WASN'T A SPRAWLING CLUB, BUT ITS LAYOUT MADE up for the lack of size. The main room was square, with a long bar on one side. A DJ booth was directly across from the bar and a dance floor was in the center. Outside the dance floor was a sprinkling of dark tables. A long hallway led to a set of bathrooms and a locked door to access the basement. The best part and one of the biggest draws to the club was the loft. Above the dance floor and chaos below, was a loft. A small bar was tucked into a corner. A couple of tables were scattered around, making it the perfect spot for a somewhat quiet conversation. It also allowed the two vampires who owned the building to look down on their potential meals.

Cameron leaned on the railing, gazing at the crowded dance floor. It was an average night for the club, which was doing better than he'd ever expected. Although he wasn't much of a businessman, Sarin had some experience. Being almost 200 years old, she'd picked up a few things along the way. Cameron didn't dress the part of a club owner, but he didn't really like to dress up much, anyway. So, he stuck with a nice pair of dark jeans, the compromise he'd made with Sarin, and a black button-up shirt with the club's logo. His beard, once wild and bushy, was tightly trimmed and neat. Even his neck was free of stubble.

Since his transformation, things had changed for Cameron Snyder. First, he didn't age anymore, but his body somehow *shifted*. His boyish figure had hardened, leaving his once round face with angles. His eyes seemed to sharpen, but he still looked the same to himself. Even his stomach thinned out just slightly. The little layer of baby fat almost absorbed into him, leaving behind the faint outline of muscle. He didn't complain about that part, that was for sure. He'd always been on the chubby side and all it took for him to lose a little weight was to become an immortal being. Simple.

Cameron felt Sarin waft over to him; her scent was apples. He could feel her presence—like the air before a lightning strike.

"Looking pretty good down there," she said, taking her spot next to him at the railing. The loft wasn't busy yet, but as the night wound down, the couples would start making their way up. Everyone was looking for a piece of privacy, whether it was to use a little cocaine, or to talk discretely. Of course, the loft had its fair share of stories.

Cameron turned and faced her. It had been over two years since that fateful night in the woods, but every time he saw Sarin, his black heart fluttered just a little. She was a goddess made of flesh— dead flesh, but still flesh.

She wore a snug pair of black slacks, leaving nothing to the imagination. The dim light of the club hid a lot, but Cameron's eyes could see that she wasn't wearing panties. That wasn't out of the ordinary for her; far from it. Her shirt was identical to his, a black button-up with the club logo, but much more flattering. Sarin's full chest pushed the buttons to the limit and left small gaps, just large enough to see her black bra. No panties were one thing, but she hated not wearing a bra. Unlike her former bandmate and first child-vampire, Vee-Exx, who wore no kind of support.

"Yeah, and it's still early," Cameron said. The pulse of the music was loud, but for them, it was fine. They heard what they wanted when they wanted—another gift Cameron wasn't expecting with his transformation. His stomach rumbled. Embarrassed, he put a hand over his belly.

Sarin smiled and moved in closer. The smell of her perfume and skin drove Cameron wild, but she already knew that.

"I know," she whispered, even though it wasn't necessary. "I'm getting hungry too." Her lips brushed his ear. "I'd love to share a meal with you." Sarin's hand went to the front of his jeans, feeling the growing bulge. "You know I love a good *meal*." She clicked her teeth together in his ear.

Cameron turned and they were almost nose to nose. He smiled and was thankful he was wearing dark jeans. Sarin had released his cock, but the erection wasn't going anywhere. He put his hand around her waist and his lips to her ear. "I have something to feed you," he said, biting her earlobe.

Sarin sighed and pushed him away, knowing he'd be thinking about her the entire night.

"Down, boy," she said, giving him a playfully stern look. Her eyes were downcast, and her lips pouted. "Find me dinner and then we'll have dessert." The sound of glass breaking grabbed their attention.

Sarin and Cameron looked towards the bar, watching Mickey clean up the broken glass.

"Let me mingle," she said, squeezing his arm. "Maybe I'll find us something to eat."

Cameron could still feel the cold flesh of Sarin's touch on his own. He watched her walk away, taking in the delicious curves of her body. His lust was almost as intense as his hunger for blood. He hoped to satiate both of them by the night's end.

"Sorry, Sarin," Mickey said as he swept the glass into a dustpan.

Sarin smiled and said, "Oh, not a problem. We have plenty left and I've wanted to replace them with plastic anyway." She surveyed the bar, watching Katelyn, her other bartender, serve the waiting customers.

"Ow, fuck," Mickey said, holding his bleeding thumb up. "That fucking hurt." He was examining his wounded finger as a red pearl of blood rose from the cut. He reached up and grabbed a few bar napkins. Mickey wrapped his finger but still winced. "I think there's still glass in there," he said, pulling the gory napkins away. The dim light of the club didn't help, but he looked anyway.

Sarin stared. She watched the thick, delicious blood ooze from his finger and salivated. Her fangs begged to be unleashed. They willed her to tear into his flesh and drink his blood. She wanted to see that glorious look of fear knowing his death was imminent.

"I'm going to run to the bathroom, okay?" he asked, still holding his injured thumb.

Sarin said nothing, just stared. The blood, the sound of his pulse, and the smell in the air made her stomach twinge. She would need to feed and soon.

"Sarin?" Mickey asked again, breaking her trance.

Sarin put the thoughts of ripping her employee's throat out and feasting on his gore from her mind.

"Sorry about that," she said. "I guess I spaced out a little." She shook her head for dramatics. "There, head's clear. But, yes, get cleaned up. I'll run the bar for a few minutes."

"Thank you," he said. Mickey took the dustpan with the broken glass and walked toward the bathroom.

A group of four customers came up to the bar, already laughing and having a good time.

"Hi, what can I get for you?" Sarin asked with a big smile on her face. The guy in front, leading the small group, had his arms around the shoulders of the two women. He may have had his arms busy, but his eyes focused on Sarin's chest. She could feel his gaze—the touch of his glare undressing her, fucking her with his eyes. He did not know what she would do to him.

"Yeah, we're gonna have three shots of tequila. *Well* tequila, no top shelf stuff, please."

Big fucking spender, Sarin thought as she reached for the cheaper alcohol.

"And my buddy back here," the guy nodded to another man standing behind them. "He's just gonna have a soda."

"Ah, yeah, a club soda with a lime wedge, please," the guy in the back said. He stepped forward and nudged the trio out of his way. He looked side-eyed at his friends and then back to Sarin. Instantly, they locked eyes.

Sarin could smell the drugs on the other three. They were tainted and soon to be even worse, with shitty alcohol flooding their bloodstreams. She didn't mind eating a drunk, but clean blood was always better. It usually wasn't an issue; she and Cameron didn't like to feed close to the bar often, but there was always an exception. This night would be an exception; she already knew it.

The young man had kind eyes and even through the reflection of his glasses, Sarin knew he was a hopeless romantic. She stared at him for just a moment longer. His posture changed as he was softening, melting almost. Their gaze was a physical thing, and she knew she had him. Her glamor was a thing to behold; when she wanted to, she could trap almost anyone.

Will you walk into my parlor? Said the spider to the fly.

"Coming right up," Sarin said, releasing her mental grasp on the man. She expertly poured the drinks and set them on the bar.

"Thank you," the man with the club soda said. He handed the shots to the other three, who quickly sent them down their waiting throats.

"Designated driver?" Sarin asked, just as the man was mid-sip.

He quickly swallowed as his friends grimaced at the crude alcohol. "Yeah, it was my turn, so..." he trailed off as the other guy kissed one of the women. The second woman stared and watched but didn't have any jealousy in her eyes. Instead, she looked full of lust.

Sarin's face split into a predatory grin, akin to a fox. "That stinks, but I'm sure you'll still have a good time." She absently wiped the bar, leaning closer to the man. Her scent was clean and robust, wafting towards him.

He closed his eyes, almost as if in a trance, and breathed deep. It was like a long blink, but it seemed like a wonderful nap to him.

"I hope so," he said, his eyes back open. He lifted the drink in a salute. "Thank you. Let me go wrangle them up. I'm sure we'll be back soon."

Sarin watched him go. She could almost taste his blood on her lips and feel the warmth of it in her belly.

"I'm all patched up," a voice said to Sarin's side.

She turned, hating the fact Mickey snuck up on her. The thought of a meal left her in a daze, thinking about the fresh blood soon to come.

Mickey held up a bandaged thumb. "Good as new and there wasn't any glass in there."

Sarin shot him a smile, the thought of his blood still fresh in her mind. "Good to hear," she said, leaving the bar and melting into the swirling throng of people.

Cameron was still in the loft, which had a decent crowd forming. He watched Sarin climb the steps.

Sarin took her spot next to him. Together, they looked down on the crowd.

The DJ had the music turned up, and the bass vibrated in the air. The energy of the music had everyone in a frenzy. Young bodies writhed together on the dance floor. Made-up faces, tight clothes, the smell of cologne and pheromones and fake smiles flashed under the multi-colored lights.

"See anything interesting down there?" Cameron asked. He watched the crowd, trying to keep his mind off the gallons of hot blood sloshing below him.

Sarin turned to him and licked her lips. The wet sound of her mouth, her luscious mouth, grabbed Cameron's attention. "Oh, I think so. I have a feeling we're going to be quite full tonight."

Cameron smiled and looked back at the prey dancing the night away.

THEY'D BEEN AT THE BLACK HEART FOR ALMOST THREE HOURS. Reggie went through eight club sodas and lime, and had pissed five times already. Luke, Mandy, and Lorrie were on the dance floor, Reggie's least favorite place. Especially sober. Maybe if he had a few drinks and some ecstasy but not sober.

He sat at a table, guarding the girls' purses and watching them grind in a vulgar display of 'dancing.' Reggie pulled his phone from his pocket and checked the time. It was almost one in the morning and he was feeling it. He stifled a yawn with his hand and heard Lorrie squeal over the booming music. Luke had buried his face in her neck, and Mandy looked on, waiting for her turn. Reggie knew they each took two more pills, washing them down with the cheap alcohol they'd consumed the entire night.

Luke pulled away from Lorrie's neck and kissed Mandy deeply. His tongue looked like it was halfway down her throat. Reluctantly, he released her, leaving a trail of saliva connecting their mouths. He turned his gaze to Lorrie, who was grinding against his thigh. Luke put his hand on the back of her head and guided her waiting mouth towards Mandy's. The two women locked eyes, gave each other a little grin and kissed.

"Tough night," someone said next to Reggie.

He jumped and turned, watching the bartender from earlier slither into a vacant seat. She had a fresh drink in her hand and put it down in front of him.

"Oh, ah, thank you," Reggie said, looking at her. Her eyes, those deep pools he'd almost drowned in earlier, were calling him again, beckoning him for another swim, this time into deep waters. Deep waters where the sharks swam and feasted on flesh and blood.

"My pleasure," she said. The music was still booming, but the angle of the speakers made talking at the tables a little easier than on the dance floor. She had to speak loud but not scream.

"Reggie," he said, holding out his hand.

"Sarin," she said.

Her hand was icy, like shaking with a corpse, but it wasn't unpleasant. When she pulled her hand back, Reggie longed for it.

"Sorry," she said. "I was scooping ice before I came over." She smiled and looked down.

Reggie sensed her coyness and had the chance to play the good guy.

"Oh, not a problem. It actually," Reggie paused, wondering if he'd come off as creepy or not, "felt pretty good." *Yup, that was creepy,* he thought. "I mean, it's so hot in here." Now it was his turn to be embarrassed.

Sarin giggled and smiled. "I know what you mean."

"Hey, buddy," Luke said as he grabbed Reggie's shoulders from behind. "Who's your new friend?"

Reggie turned and saw the sweaty faces of his friends. Luke was flushed and his crown was damp, but he looked like he was having a great time. He didn't even try to hide the fact he had an erection, which wasn't very impressive. Maybe the drugs and booze made him oblivious, but it wasn't hard to notice. Lorrie and Mandy were whispering and shooting dirty looks at Sarin. Each glare and whisper was followed by some groping and laughing.

"Um, this is Sarin," Reggie told Luke, who was thoroughly eye-fucking her. "She works here."

"Oh, very nice," Luke was dialing up the charm as he pushed past Reggie and stood in front of Sarin. "How very nice to meet you." He held out his sweaty palm.

Sarin looked at it and ignored him. "So, Reggie, let me get back to work. Maybe I'll see you later?"

Reggie felt like he was floating. Not only had Sarin ignored Luke, but she was flirting with him. A beautiful woman, hotter than the two he'd come with, actually flirting with him. He needed to play it cool.

"Maybe, we'll see," he said with a smile. A smile he hoped was relaxed.

"You guys have a good rest of the night," she told the trio, all three staring at her.

Reggie watched her walk away, following the tightness of her ass as she moved through the crowd.

"What a cunt," Mandy said, grabbing her purse from the table. She took out her cell phone, checked it and put it back.

"Yeah, who the fuck does she think she is?" Lorrie asked, grabbing her purse as well. She took out a pack of cigarettes and a lighter. "I'm gonna have a smoke. Anyone coming?" She held them out to her friends.

"Might as well," Luke said, wrapping his arm around Mandy's waist. "Are you coming?" he asked her.

Mandy kissed his nose. "Later, and hopefully a few times."

Luke smiled. "Oh, I think I can make that happen." He squeezed her ass. "Lead the way," he told Lorrie.

Mandy took her purse and threw it over her shoulder.

Together, they pushed through the crowd and outside.

Reggie picked up his drink and sipped. The coldness of the glass reminded him of her. A chill, like being watched, ran through his body.

"Is he the one?" Cameron asked as Sarin sat at the table.

"Yup, he's the one and he's going to be delectable."

Cameron smiled, "Perfect. I'll go take care of the friends." He stood up and rubbed a crease from his shirt. He took out his cell phone and dialed a number. "Hello, yes, I need a cab at The Black Heart," he said. "Yes, three people. Yup, we'll be waiting outside. Thank you." He ended the call and tucked the phone into his pocket as he walked downstairs.

"Last call!" Mickey yelled from behind the bar. He rang an obnoxious bell on the wall behind him and screamed again. "Last call for alcohol!" he shouted. A few hisses and boos came from the crowd, but not many. The night was winding down and most people had their fill of drinking and dancing.

Cameron walked out into the night air. The coolness licked his skin, as soft and welcoming as Sarin's tongue. He listened and scanned the groups of smokers until he found them.

"—my place," the guy in the group said, before he realized Cameron was standing behind him. He turned and looked at Cameron, annoyed at the new male encroaching on his area. "Can I help you?" The guy asked, putting his cigarette in his mouth and taking a drag.

"Yes, sorry to bother you, but I'm Cameron, one of the club's owners." He pointed to his shirt with the logo on it. Instantly, he saw the other guy relax, realizing he wasn't a threat to his women.

"Oh, okay. What's up?" The guy asked, letting the cigarette hang at a jaunty angle from his lips.

"Your friend, Reggie, told me to tell you he wouldn't be driving you tonight and that he called you a cab." As if on cue, the taxi pulled up to the group.

"Really?" one woman asked. "That's not like him. Let me talk to him for a second, to be sure."

Cameron wasn't as gifted as Sarin with his glamor, but it wasn't too hard against a drunk and drugged woman. His eyes snagged hers, locking them in place.

"Trust me, he's fine," Cameron said, alternating his look to all three of them.

Slowly, like an ice cube in a bowl of soup, they melted. The walls of protection they'd built around themselves to defend against a stranger, crumbled.

"Now, why don't you three get in the cab and enjoy the rest of your night?" Cameron walked to the taxi and opened the back door.

The guy nodded. "Yeah, come on," he told the girls with a smile. "Let's go back to my place and have some fun." He took a small bag with a few pills from his pocket. "I have a couple more left."

The girls smiled and got into the car, followed by the guy.

"If you see Reggie, tell him thanks for nothing," the guy said from the car's open window.

"Sure thing," Cameron began, but the window was already

rolling up. The car sped off into the night, and Cameron smiled. His fangs itched, but he knew soon they'd be soaked in blood.

REGGIE WALKED THROUGH THE DARK STREET, LOOKING FOR HIS CAR. He was pissed. He couldn't believe his friends left without him. Not only that, but they didn't even say anything. They just up and disappeared. He called each of their cell phones numerous times, but he had an idea of what they were doing. That made it even worse. He'd hoped to at least mess around with Lorrie, but Luke wasn't having that. Some fucking friend.

Reggie stuffed his hands in his pants pockets and walked. The streetlights, which had been on when they'd arrived, were dull, and some were even out. It didn't matter; he was sure he remembered where his car was. He pulled his keys out of his pocket and clicked the 'lock' button on the fob. In the distance, he heard the horn beep and could see a quick flash of headlights. He couldn't get there fast enough.

A cool breeze blew a discarded cigarette wrapper and other trash against Reggie's shoes in a whirlwind. He shivered. The coolness against his skin made him think of her: Sarin, the woman in the bar with the icy touch. Reggie shivered again, not from the breeze but from the memory of her skin. The slick cold of her flesh.

His car was in view as he approached the mouth of a dark alleyway to his right. Reggie stopped when he heard something shuffle in the darkness.

"Going home alone?" a voice asked from the gloom.

Reggie's heart was racing. At first, he was nervous, wondering what beasts lurked in the shadows. The illogical fear of the dark that is inanely possessed by all humans, regardless of age. His heart was still fluttering, but for another reason—he knew that voice.

Sarin stepped out of the darkness. It seemed to pull at her, moving like oil draped around her skin.

Reggie stood staring at the gothic beauty. She was gorgeous in the club lighting, but in the moon's light, she was ethereal. A pale ghost dripping lust and wanting. And did he ever want her? His eyes drank the curves of her body, admiring her round hips and the fullness of her chest. When he found her face, he was entranced. The attraction was more than physical; it felt almost magnetic. He knew he would follow her into the alleyway, but why? That was a mystery, but he didn't care. If she told him, at that moment, to play in traffic, he would. She'd asked him something—a question. She'd asked him a question. His mind raced, hoping to save face with her, to prolong the interaction.

"Yes," he blurted out, a little louder than he'd intended. Reggie cleared his throat and took a step closer to her. "I mean, yeah, my asshole friends ditched me." He kicked at a cigarette butt on the ground, grinding it with his toe. "So, now I'll head home and go to bed…I guess." Reggie looked up at her, doing his best to look slightly desperate but alluring. He didn't think he'd hit the mark, but it was worth a try.

"Oh, that sucks," she said, taking another step back into the gloom. "I was just taking the trash out and saw you. You looked lonely." She smiled at him, which made *him* smile. "And a little sad." Sarin gave him a mock pout.

Reggie took a step towards her and another. It was like he was in her gravitational pull. Her eyes kept him locked in. Even when he broke the gaze, his brain screamed to look at her again.

"Well, I hope you had a good time tonight, Mr. Club soda and Lime," she smirked and licked her lips, taking another step back. Then, the shadows completely enveloped her, leaving only the faint outline of her pale skin visible. And then, she was gone.

Reggie stepped forward, his toes on the edge of the darkness. Something shifted in the shadows and creaked, like a dog stretching.

"Sarin?" he asked. His bravado was fading. Fear of the darkness and creatures of the night was creeping in, slipping past her hold over him. But, it wasn't enough. Reggie walked into the dark alley. "Do you need help?" Nothing, no answer. Reggie dug into his pocket and pulled out his cell phone. The screen's backlight was blinding, but he clicked on the flashlight app. "Sarin," he gasped, holding the light out before him, warding off shadows.

Sarin stood there, motionless. Her head was down, and her hair hung low, covering her face.

"A-are you okay?" Reggie asked, stepping closer. He reached out to touch her. "Sarin? Please, are you okay?"

A low growl rumbled from the woman's throat. It wasn't quite canine in its sound, but it was far from human. Very far.

Sarin lifted her head slowly.

Reggie's brain was struggling to comprehend what was in front of him. The synapses were firing hard, trying to tell his legs to fucking run, that the thing in front of him wasn't safe. That message never arrived.

Sarin was a nightmare made of flesh, bone and teeth. The once beautiful woman was no more—her delicate, innocent face was an unholy abomination. Once pouty and very kissable, her mouth now split wide, seeming to go to her ears. Her jaw had widened and her face lengthened. It had to enlarge to fit all of those teeth. Her mouth was sharklike, full of rows of teeth, and deadly. Sarin's fingers, which he previously hoped to see wrapped around his cock, were now long and tipped in black claws.

Reggie shook, praying the message from his brain to his legs would get there. Get there and fast. Finally, he felt his body moving, turning away from the beast in the shadows coming toward him. Reggie spun, seeking freedom and the light of the moon.

A hand, another one tipped in claws, grabbed his throat when he turned. The face of a man—well, what used to be a man—stared at him. The man's mouth opened wide, showing rows of seemingly never-ending teeth.

CAMERON WATCHED REGGIE WALK INTO THE SHADOWY ALLEY, knowing it was the last thing he'd ever do. He went from being a man, to being food, in an instant. Cameron could hear him talking to Sarin, even around the corner, near the parking lot. It was time and not a moment too soon; he was starving.

Cameron's movement was silent as he crept up behind Reggie. He felt himself changing under the moonlight and loved it. He'd been scared the first few times he took his vampiric form, not knowing what it would feel like and shirking at the slight discomfort. Now, he relished it. The little creaks and cracks were welcoming. Even the pain was pleasant, like having slightly sore muscles after a long day of hard work. Cameron's eyes pierced the gloom of the alley as he stared at Reggie's neck—his wonderous neck full of lifeblood. Salty and nourishing, it sang to him. It willed him to open the throat and feast. To feast and then fuck.

Sarin stood in front of the man, her hair hanging low. Cameron knew she'd already changed; he noticed her fingers, which weren't illuminated by the man's weak flashlight.

Cameron heard him talking but didn't pay attention. All he could hear was the growling in his belly—the craving for blood and death.

The moment of truth was coming and Cameron licked his fangs, his wicked instruments of murder. The man sprung, running from Sarin. He almost caught Cameron off guard. Almost. Cameron reached up and seized the man's throat. The pulse raced under his undead fingers, making him drool. He looked at the fear in Reggie's eyes, and just a hint of his former human pity made him hesitate. Sarin ended that quickly.

She attacked first, losing her patience. Her mouth wrapped around the right side of Reggie's neck and bit. Bone and flesh were severed and a gout of hot blood flooded her mouth.

Cameron watched her eyes roll back as she fed and knew he needed to bite before she drained the man. He released his hand, but Sarin's claws were dug into Reggie's abdomen, holding him up. Cameron bit the other side of the neck. His reward was a rush of blood—salty and delicious. His and Sarin's lips were touching as they each bit harder, willing more blood from the corpse.

The flow stopped. Sarin looked at Cameron, their mouths still attached to Reggie's neck. The feeding was over, but a new carnal desire was growing like a raging fire. She pulled her top fangs from the man's neck and allowed her tongue to slither. Sarin licked Cameron's mouth, stealing a few drops of errant blood.

He smiled, still with his teeth in the man's dead flesh. Cameron felt himself hardening. He knew what came next. Feeding was great; it kept them 'alive,' but the fucking...the fucking was what made him *feel* alive.

Cameron clamped his jaws hard, half-severing the man's neck. He spat the flesh and bone onto the alley floor. He looked at Sarin with a different hunger in his eyes. Blood ran down his lips—the final bite had given him another burst.

Sarin released her jaws, letting the head flop to the side. Wet meat and gristle shone in the moonlight. Bright to the eyes of the vampires. Her claws were still buried in Reggie's corpse and she picked him up like nothing. Sarin flipped open the lid of the dumpster and tossed him in. Now Cameron had her full attention.

"Fuck me," she growled, lunging at him. Sarin's fangs were still out, as were Cameron's. Their grotesque mouths met in passion—two beasts of death and legend. Their tongues tangled, seeking the remaining blood left by their partners. Sarin's claws wound into Cameron's hair and she pulled his head back, breaking their kiss. "I said, fuck me," she hissed. Her free hand grabbed at his cock, which was begging to be released.

Cameron smiled wide, licking his lips. He grabbed Sarin's hips and pushed her away.

"You fucking want it?" He retook her hips.

"Yes," she breathed.

The smell of her breath, sweet and bloody, put Cameron over the edge. He turned Sarin around and pushed her roughly into the wall.

Her face hit the bricks and she moaned. There was no pain, only lust. Sarin's fingers, which were human again, fumbled at her pants.

She knew Cameron would rip them off if she didn't get them down fast.

Cameron clawed at her waistline, pulling at the stubborn fabric. He bit at her cold neck, nipping her flesh with his fangs. His cock glistened, and he was tearing her pants if she didn't get her pussy out soon.

Finally, Sarin's pants were down, at least far enough for them. She put her hands against the brick wall and arched her back.

Cameron grabbed her hips with his left hand and guided his cock with his right.

Sarin's sex was dripping, welcoming him to fill her.

Cameron obliged and hissed at the cool tightness of her vagina.

She pushed back, taking him abruptly to the base. Together, they found their rhythm and fucked under the moon's light.

ANOTHER PREDATOR WAS OUT THAT NIGHT—ANOTHER HUNTER OF flesh. Sarin and Cameron didn't see him, and that was the point. It was his job not to be seen but to see. And see, he did.

The alley's darkness was too thick for his camera to penetrate, even with the fancy lens. It didn't matter; he had enough evidence, at least he hoped.

When the crazy old man had first called him to stake out a nightclub, he'd taken the job. It was easy money and since retiring from the police department, he needed a hobby. Becoming a private investigator was the most logical choice. It wasn't a dangerous job, although two brothers had been killed a few years back. But, they were rookies, too gung-ho, rushing into things. No, not him. Not Sgt. Rick Hendrickson. He was smart. He observed from a distance with a long lens and a hot cup of coffee.

The job had been simple at first. Watch the club owners, and snap pictures of them when possible, but do not interfere. That was key. Regardless of what he saw or captured, to not call the police. His payment depended on it.

For weeks, nothing had happened. Rick took a few blurry pictures here and there, sending them back to the employer, whose name he'd never even received.

A rather boring job, until tonight.

Rick spent too many years as a cop and his instincts were still too sharp. He knew something terrible would happen when that kid walked into the alley. When he saw the woman, Sarin, standing at the mouth of the darkness, like a fucking ghoul. A logical person would think it was a hookup, a quick fuck, letting the night hide their fun. But he knew differently. Especially when the other owner, Cameron, walked in behind the guy.

Rick had pictures of it all. Of course, they were blurry, but the boss didn't care. He hoped this would be enough to get him paid and off this fucking job.

4

HUNTING THE HUNTERS

IT HAD BEEN four days since John received the pictures from his PI, Rick. They were the same as before, but there'd been another person this time—a young man.

The blue light of the laptop hurt his eyes, and Marne had bought him blue-blocker glasses, but he didn't want to wear them. The pain of the screen was his penance, his payment for not killing them faster. And now, another life was probably lost to the fucking monsters.

It was still dark, but the sun was starting to pinken the sky in the east. Marne wasn't due for another hour, but he didn't care. He hadn't been eating much; when he did, it was usually take-out. He would never fire her, no. She did plenty for him, especially cleaning. He could fend for himself with food, but he despised cleaning. He also knew her job was a significant source of income for her growing family, so she stayed.

John refreshed the browser and rechecked the news. He brought up every local news page in the area of The Black Heart, hoping for a lead, and praying for confirmation. He was so close.

A few weeks ago, a homeless man was found dead by the train

tracks, not far from the club. It looked obvious that he'd been killed by the train, but John had his feelers out to as many medical examiners as he could find. His grandmother would've called it the luck of the Irish, but he called it having a shit ton of money. Typically, a train accident is pretty straightforward and cut and dry. But this one caught the observant eye of the police and the ME. The man was undoubtedly hit by the train, but when the pieces of him were gathered and put back together, it was a different story.

First, at the crime scene, there was minimal blood. He could've been killed by the train and dragged until his corpse was finally pulled under and dismembered. That was the first sign to the ME that something was odd. It was possible but unlikely. When he'd examined the body, he quickly realized it was almost entirely devoid of blood. Even when scattered by a train, the body would still contain something, anything to let you know. Not in this case. And then there were the marks. The flesh had been severely shredded from the accident, but there were marks on the neck and inner thigh. Strange damage, not caused by a train, but more closely resembled an animal bite. So, of course, the ME put it down as a John Doe killed by a train. That's what his bosses wanted and he was happy to fall in line. But not before he did a *separate* report and took his pictures.

When John found those pictures and that report in his email, he'd nearly had a heart attack. For two years, the trail had gone cold looking for the vampires. He figured they left the country, or were laying low. Now, he'd had a glimmer of hope, something to go on.

Hiring Rick, the PI, was the next step, but he wouldn't make the same mistake again. He'd use the man to find them, confirm his suspicions, and then call in professionals. Not a couple of kids with a history of vampire hunting in their past, but fucking pros. Men and women who killed monsters, who hunted them and knew the danger. That search had been a little more complicated. There was no listing for *vampire hunters* in the phonebook. But, again, lots of money helped.

The last step was the body. John was confident it was them, especially with the blurred pictures, but he needed a body. It was days since the young man had been seen with them, but nothing was in the news. There were no signs of a dead man or cases of a missing person. It was the last step before the call could be made.

John sipped at his coffee and refreshed the page.

There! It was there. He read and re-read the headline before scanning the article.

LOCAL MAN FOUND DEAD

HE KNEW IT WAS THE YOUNG MAN FROM THE PICTURES. THE PAPER said the body of a 23-year-old man, whose identity was being withheld, was found in a dumpster. It was being treated as a homicide, but the possibility of an animal attack wasn't being ruled out. More would be covered in the coming hours.

John felt sick and satisfied at once. His hands trembled as he picked up his phone. He opened the keypad; the number wasn't saved. John dialed international and listened to the phone ring.

SALIM OSBOURNE FELT HIS PHONE VIBRATING IN HIS COAT POCKET. HE watched Polly push their son on the swings.

"Daddy, look at me," Ahmed shrieked as he catapulted into the air, higher and higher.

Polly braced to regain her son's momentum, launching him even further into the sky.

"Weeeee," the boy shrieked. His little hands gripped the chains on the swing tight. He leaned forward, letting the sun warm his olive skin.

Salim smiled. It was one of the most beautiful things he'd seen, and he had never felt more in love. To watch his wife and the mother of his son happy again was a joy. They never told Ahmed he would be a big brother; after last month, they wouldn't have to.

Polly knew something was wrong with the baby. She told Salim a few days before the miscarriage, but still, she held out hope. At night, she'd pray with her grandmother's rosary beads clutched tight in her fists. Unfortunately, her prayers fell on deaf ears.

Salim wanted to pray with her, even if he thought it was bullshit, but he couldn't. He knew monsters existed in the world. Too many nightmares stalked the earth. What kind of God would allow that? In his life, some had called him a monster too. A beast, a killer, a gun for hire. The things he did. No, he wasn't going to pray. If anything, God would strike him down for making a request.

Things were settling down, and life was getting on. Polly had a few tough weeks in bed, and dealing with a 3-year-old boy wasn't helping. Salim did what he could, but bills needed to be paid and food put on the table. Finally, Polly was able to overcome, which he knew she would. Whether it was through prayer or the modern medicine of prescription pills, she made it.

Ahmed was none the wiser. He just thought mommy was sick and sleepy, which in a way, she was. He went to pre-school for an hour every other day, watched his shows, and took naps. To him, life was good.

Salim waved to his son, but the phone hadn't stopped ringing. It was an itch—an itch he needed to scratch. He didn't have many friends, and they sure as shit wouldn't be calling him on a Tuesday afternoon. It was work. It was always work. He pulled the phone from his pocket and felt his heart drop.

It was a call from America. He never saved a number on his phone, but his memory was impeccable. He hadn't seen the number in quite some time, but he remembered it. His skin felt clammy, despite the sea breeze off the English Channel. Salim was just getting his life back in order, but he knew this could be his big shot. No more bullshit jobs of breaking fingers for loan sharks, torching buildings, or even murders. He figured there would be killing with this job, but killing vampires was just work. And he was good at it.

Salim's thumb hovered over the green button on the phone. He looked up at Polly and Ahmed, so lost in their little world, a world he never truly felt a part of. Salim answered.

"Hello?" he said. His accent wasn't entirely British, even though he'd spent the better part of his adult life in the country. Just a little bit on his "h", but that was it.

"Oh, thank God," John said on the other line. "I thought you'd changed your number or fucking died."

No, just my unborn child. I'm still kicking, Salim thought.

"Nope, just out with my wife and son," he waved to Polly, looking at him with a scowl. "So, let's make this quick, shall we."

John cleared his throat. "Of course, of course. I'm too excited and want to get this done immediately." There was a sound of a keyboard clicking. "Salim, my friend, I've found them. And they're not going anywhere." He stammered and then exclaimed, "But I still need this done now. No more waiting, no more delays. I need you and your people on a plane to the US, tonight if possible."

Salim sighed. He knew that was going to be the issue—the old man, stuck in his American ways. He needed things done immediately. No waiting. No concern for anyone's life or family. No, John had money, he was important and was never told no.

"I'm not sure if that's doable, John," Salim said, holding up his pointer finger to let Polly know he'd be off the phone in a minute.

"Sure, it is." There was more clicking on the keyboard. "I can have a private jet chartered for you at any airport by," he paused, "10pm, your time."

Salim looked at his watch. It was just past noon. "John, most of my people aren't even in the UK anymore—they're scattered into the wind. They're not far, but getting them together will take some time."

John was silent. Salim heard the man mumbling like he was talking to himself.

Salim was doing mental calculations in his head. The equipment he had, so that wasn't an issue. But it was gathering the rest of them. The price needed to be high to entice them to drop what they were doing, board a plane for the States and hunt two, if not three, vampires.

"I can get them here," Salim said, "but not for three days."

John sighed and started to speak, but Salim cut him off.

"John, this won't be cheap, you know that, right?" Salim was thinking of the money in his head. This man had somehow found him almost a year ago. That in itself was an accomplishment and probably took at least six figures to do. He had money, that was for sure.

"Name it," John said.

Salim didn't want to scare the man away, but he didn't think that was possible. He knew desperation when he heard it.

"Two million, US. Each." Salim's heart was racing. That was life-changing money. Breaking fingers didn't pay as much as he'd like.

"Done," John spat without hesitation. "And 50k for additional expenses."

"Half now and a half when the job is complete. I'll bring you their black hearts myself."

"Get me account numbers, and the money will be wired within an hour. I'll be there with you," John told him. "I won't interfere, but I want to watch them die—to suffer. To burn in the purifying light of day."

Polly was walking towards Salim with Ahmed's hand in hers.

Salim rushed. "Perfect. I'll make some calls, and you'll hear back from me by tonight." Polly stopped in front of him. He mouthed, *sorry* to her.

"Great, I'll be waiting," John said.

Salim hung up without saying goodbye. He had some news for his wife.

MARY DANNER AWOKE WITH HAIR IN HER MOUTH AND A RAGING hangover. She hoped the hair was hers. Although, after the last few times, she'd awakened in a fog not sure what to expect.

The smell of her shampoo and the subtle taste of vomit gave her a mix of relief and disgust. Her eyes remained closed. She knew opening them would allow the brutal light of the day in. She heard a shrill sound in the depths of her slowly awakening mind. It was penetrating, boring into her skull and brain. The pain of her hang-over was growing, and her mouth tasted like shit. She groaned and reached out for her phone, which was still ringing. She hated her ringtone, but knew she'd sleep right through it if she had something pleasant. Mary felt the vibration under her searching fingers. She grabbed it and pulled it in front of her face. Finally, Mary opened her eyes.

Midday light was assaulting, and her vision was out of focus. She struggled to keep her eyes open. Closing them might help to dull the pain in the back of her eyeballs. But she couldn't. She knew this was a work call and she needed the money.

Mary's social life was non-existent and hadn't been much before becoming a nun. But, since being disavowed, it became even worse.

From the day she entered the convent, she knew a life devoted to God wasn't the way. But, Mary's dying mother made her swear an oath to be a servant of God. That didn't last long. She tried, oh God, did she try, but in the end, it wasn't for her. The day she took the habit, she cried. It had been a life sentence for her—a life of service to the Lord and no one else. She wasn't much in the dating depart-ment, but she was still a woman. A woman that occasionally enjoyed the company of men. That was no longer an option. Or so she thought. Being a nun didn't last long. Leaving wasn't an option; she wasn't a quitter. No, she needed to be left with no choice. To be forced into leaving the habit behind and told she could never come back. That night, she'd been caught; she knew that was it. The congregation convened the following day and her act, so heinous, warranted a petition to the bishop for immediate excommunication.

The day the priory doors closed behind her, Mary breathed a

sigh of relief. Yet, she was overcome with fear and shame. She'd failed her mother. Mary, once again, felt like a failure. For days she wandered, riding trains around Europe, blowing her money and drinking herself to oblivion. Mary knew her death wouldn't be far behind. She ended up in many unsavory bars and parts of town. The people she associated with and the drugs and alcohol she put into her body were killing her. That was until she met him.

He was tan, with black hair and dusky eyes. His accent was a mixture of American with a bit of UK. Mary was drunk, smoking a cigarette in an Irish pub. It had gone out, but she held the filter with two inches of ash hanging off it. He slid into her booth with a beer in one hand and water in the other. He put the water in front of her and took the cigarette from her hand. He put it in the ashtray next to a half-dozen others.

"Do you know who I am?" he asked, pushing the water closer.

"No," she slurred. Mary took the straw and pulled the paper from the top of it. She drank half in one gulp. "But I have a feeling you're going to tell me."

He smiled and sipped his beer. A pair of dark eyes locked onto her watery blue ones. "I have a proposition for you, Mary," he said, setting his glass down.

Mary looked at him and spat a lemon seed into the cup. "I'm not a fucking whore," she blurted. It drew a few glares from the other bar patrons and a few laughs, but that was it.

The man smiled at her and opened both of his hands. "Mary, I would never think that, nor is that what I'm looking for." He put his hands together as if in prayer. "I know about your history, your background." He leaned closer to her. The smell of cigarettes and alcohol wafted from her mouth. "About the priory."

Mary's eyes narrowed and she stared back at him. She was hundreds of miles from that place, yet this man in front of her knew. She could see it in his eyes.

"I know about that night, Mary. That night…what you did." He was staring at her, not breaking his gaze.

Mary looked away. Her face burned with shame. Her nose stung and she was going to cry.

"Yeah, well, fuck you too," she muttered. Mary dug through her purse and pulled out her pack of cigarettes. She lit one and was preparing to leave. "Thanks for ruining my night, asshole." Tears were running down her cheeks. If she had worn makeup, it would've been smeared and running.

"Mary, sit," he demanded.

She stopped mid-stride and froze. She didn't like being told what to do, but something about this strange man had her captivated. Mary licked her lips; the cigarette pinched between her fingers. Then, slowly, she sat back down. Mary ashed in the tray and took a drag.

"I know and I don't care. It's what drew me to you. The tenacity, the desire, the fight against authority and even your push against evil."

Mary smoked. Her tears seemed a thing of the past and she even felt slightly sober. It could be the fact she was sitting still and not moving, but she didn't know. This mysterious man made her feel *different*. There was something about him.

He took his pack of cigarettes out and lit one. "Would you like to hear my proposition now?"

Mary smoked and stared. "Sure, but could we start with a name? You know mine." She laughed, smoke shooting from her mouth. "You know quite a bit about me."

He puffed and smiled, letting the smoke flow from his lips. "Me, my name is Salim and I hunt monsters."

Mary flashed back to the present and looked at the name on the screen. Then, she touched the green icon to answer the call.

"What?" Mary mumbled into the phone.

Salim laughed. "And good morning to you," he paused. "Never mind, I guess I should say good afternoon."

Mary sat up, clutching the phone to her ear. She grabbed a half-empty bottle of lukewarm water and drank. Mary squeezed every drop and tossed it.

"Yeah, yeah," she said, smacking her lips in the phone. She scanned for another drink, alcohol or not, but was unsuccessful.

"I have a job for you," Salim said. His voice started off soft and pleasant, taking on a serious edge. "And Mary, this is the big one, a game changer. A fucking career maker, Mary. This isn't some bull-shit wild goose chase. And if it is, who fucking cares. The pay is worth it, trust me."

Mary's head throbbed, but the excitement in Salim's voice had her on edge. "What kind of money?"

"Can you take the job?" he asked, ignoring her question.

Mary was silent. During their last job, she'd almost died. A stray bullet, meant for the vampire they were hunting, grazed her ribs. The follow-up rounds subdued the beast, allowing them to kill it. That had been over a year earlier. Fuck it. What did she have to live for?

"Yeah, I can fucking take it." Mary found a bottle of aspirin. She shook out four tablets and threw them into her mouth. They were bitter, adding to the awful taste already living on her tongue. She dry swallowed, feeling them the entire way down.

"Great. But, Mary, I need you in top shape. So get the drinking out of your system now. Our flight leaves in a few days."

Mary swallowed again. It felt like the pills had lodged in her throat.

"Flight? Where are we going?"

"America, Mary."

"Vampires in America? We haven't killed one there. At least I haven't."

Salim laughed in her ear. "Well, my dear, there's a first time for everything." He paused. "Now, get ready. I'm sending a car for you in two hours. Check your email. There will be a train ticket sched-uled for tonight. It'll bring you to England. The rest of the team is on their way. Mary, this is the big one. We can fucking retire after this, I'm telling you."

"Yeah, you keep saying that, but I don't have a number yet, now do I, Salim?"

There was silence on the line. "Two million...each." He let it hang in the air.

Mary was silent. He wasn't kidding; that was life-changing money for sure. Something she never thought was possible. Of course, killing things that weren't supposed to exist was supposed to pay well, but until that call, nothing had compared. Not even close.

"Two hours. Be ready and somewhat sober."

The line went dead.

DAYS LATER, SALIM SAT IN THE BACK OF AN SUV THAT COST AS MUCH as his first house. It wasn't his, but with the money he was going to make, it someday could be. Anxiously, he checked his watch. The other three members of his team weren't late, yet. He always grew up with the mantra that fifteen minutes was on time, on time was late, and late was unacceptable. He'd been a half hour early for their flight to the US.

"Here they come," his driver, whose name he hadn't learned, said.

Salim looked through the thick tint of the windows as another vehicle—a stretch limousine—approached.

"Thank you," Salim said to the driver and got out of the vehicle.

The tarmac was breezy, but it felt good. The air conditioning in the car was making him shiver and his nose felt like it was drying out. The wind was cool, but mostly comfortable. A small jet growled as the pilots warmed it up and completed pre-flight checks.

Salim grabbed his bags from the back of the car and stood watching the limo as it approached.

The sleek, black vehicle slowed to a stop and Salim strained to see through the tint. He hoped it contained the rest of his team. Arthur and Paolo were reliable, but Mary could have her moments. When he'd called, she still sounded drunk, which wasn't out of the realm of possibility, even though it was midday or so. But, no, Salim had faith in her. Not so much in her ability to stay sober but her lust for the death of evil and, of course, a big payday. She'd be in the car —he knew it.

The limo door opened, and the two men, his hunters, stepped out.

Arthur was thin and the suit he wore was two sizes too big. He buttoned it up as the wind whipped the bottom of his jacket. His reddish hair was close-cropped and his eyes were squinted. A few days' worth of stubble shadowed his face, which was normal for him.

Paolo was opposite to his counterpart: squat, with a deep olive complexion and a buzz cut. Fancy clothes weren't his thing. He wore a snug pair of jeans and a button-up shirt, which was partially open. He had shaved for the occasion, which helped highlight the scar on his left cheek.

Salim held his breath. There weren't any more vehicles approaching and Mary hadn't stepped out yet. He watched and saw the driver, who stood outside the car, extend his hand to the open door.

From the maw of the vehicle came a hand. The driver took it and helped Mary out onto the tarmac.

She looked good, much better than Salim remembered. And he and Mary had some *fond* memories together.

Mary wore almost as tight of jeans as Paolo's and a graphic t-shirt. Her naturally blonde hair was in a loose ponytail that seemed to lay the right way. Even her eyes, which Salim was used to seeing cloudy with intoxication, were clear. She looked around and found him and smiled.

Salim felt his pulse quicken. He had to remind himself he was a married man with a child. He hoped that was enough.

"It's about time," Salim said, walking over to his team. He shook their hands, except for Mary, whom he hugged.

"Yeah, yeah," muttered Arthur. "I'm sure you were here at the crack of dawn. Salim, you won't even be late for your funeral."

Salim looked at him with a questioning glance. He wasn't sure if that was quite the saying, but he didn't care.

"Come on," Salim said. "Let's get on board and get going." He began wheeling his luggage towards the plane.

"No, sir. We'll get that," his driver, who was now out of the car, said.

Salim looked at him and nodded. "Thank you." He looked back at his team. Their luggage was being unloaded as well. "Okay then, let's check this plane out, shall we?"

The pilot stood at the top of the steps and welcomed them aboard.

Paolo let out a long whistle as he looked around the jet's cabin.

"Damn, Salim, who the fuck is this guy?" He touched the smooth leather of the seats as he walked to the back of the plane.

"I'll say," said Arthur, following right behind his friend. "This is some swank right here." He examined a TV screen in the back of a seat. "Better than commercial, that's for sure."

Mary and Salim walked aboard and were taken aback.

"Very nice, very nice," Mary said with a nod. "Now, where's that drink cart?"

Salim shot her a glance.

"Kidding, kidding." Mary put her hands up and smiled. "I have a flask in my purse." This time, she wasn't joking.

Salim gave her a dirty look but knew she wasn't lying. He also knew she needed it, at least to keep her level. She was one of the best vampire hunters he'd ever seen, even if she was a little drunk. Having her quit cold turkey would be much worse than having her buzzed up.

Mary dug into her purse and pulled out a small flask. She opened it and took a quick sip. Nothing much, but enough to take the edge off.

The pilot closed up the door and fastened it. Then, he turned and looked at his guests.

"Okay, folks. Mr. Calderon insisted we get airborne as soon as possible, so if you could all take a seat and buckle up. Once we're at cruising altitude, feel free to get up. All equipment and luggage have been stowed and will be waiting for you upon landing."

The four of them listened and found seats. It wasn't difficult to do so. The plane could easily accommodate twenty-five passengers and then some, especially if some of them sat on the oversized couch against the wall.

The engines whined and powered up. Then, with a lurch, the plane shot down the runway and was in the air.

"Okay," Salim said, unbuckling once the lights had turned off, "let's get down to business, shall we?"

5

CHEESE PIZZA

CAMERON STOOD on the balcony above the dance floor. A few tables near him were occupied, but many more were open. The small bar was doing well, keeping up with the steady flow of patrons looking for a drink and a quiet place. He looked down on the few drunken people grinding on the dance floor. Their blood would be pumping and pumping hard. He could almost taste their coppery life force in his mouth. The feeling of their hot gore spraying the back of his throat as he opened a fat artery. Cameron's stomach growled.

It had been a few days since he and Sarin had killed the young man in the alley. They didn't need to feed daily, but they would experience discomfort soon. He was feeling it and knew Sarin was the same. She'd learned over the years how to control the urges and hunger, but there was only so much she could do.

The body of the young man, identified as Reginald Ingalls, was found on garbage day. The sanitation worker was shocked when the dumpster was rolled out and opened. For hours, the streets were locked down and cordoned off. Uniformed cops and plain-clothes detectives swarmed the area, but nothing concrete had been discovered.

Sarin and Cameron had answered all the detective's questions—

during night hours, obviously. They did their parts as good citizens, knowing there was no way for them to be implemented. Their DNA was nothing, blank. If a piece of their hair, or flesh was found, it would be an error when examined—their fingerprints, too. Those were a thing of the past that neither Sarin nor Cameron had use for. No, they had no fear of human law enforcement, but the crime scene came with a particular set of complications.

As a basic rule and one to keep their club a success, Sarin and Cameron didn't normally feed nearby. It was rare and few and far between. Mangled corpses in the area weren't the best for business, that was for sure. They'd gotten sloppy with Reggie. They should've torched him in his car, ripped him apart, or just waited. Instead, the predatory side of their *condition* got the best of them. Their next feeding would be different; it had to be.

Cameron watched Sarin laugh as she talked with two men. She was handing them drinks from the bar, and Cameron watched them make lewd gestures when she turned. He smirked, knowing these guys did not know what they were getting into. With drinks in hand, the two guys kept the conversation going until Sarin walked away. Like puppies, they followed her.

The trio climbed the steps, taking them to the balcony area where Cameron was. He tried not to make it obvious, but he was watching.

The lead guy sipped from his cup; his wispy mustache touched the bubbles of the soda. He wore a ridiculous graphic t-shirt at least two sizes too small, accenting his doughy midsection and man-tits. His buddy wasn't much better. He was thin, clean-shaven, and littered with acne scars and a few fresh bumps.

Cameron had seen guys like them in his high school. To most people, his old self resembled these losers. He sighed a little, knowing it was wrong to judge people on looks alone. It wasn't fair, and he fucking hated when it happened to him. Still, there was something off about them.

Sarin led the men up the stairs as if they were on a string. She stopped at the top and turned to both of them.

"Okay, fellas, I need to talk with my partner but enjoy the night. I'm sure I'll be seeing you again," she said with a wink.

Cameron tried hard not to laugh. The guys were practically drooling as they watched her walk away. She wiggled her hips just a little more than necessary to give them a show.

"New friends?" Cameron asked as she stopped next to him. The two vampires looked down on their little kingdom.

Sarin smirked. "Hardly. Just two, sad sacks looking for something to jerk off to later on."

Cameron looked over his shoulder at the two men, who'd taken one of the empty tables. They were still looking at Sarin, not caring that Cameron watched them.

"Yeah, it's a good thing you didn't have a drink. They would've drugged it for sure."

Sarin could feel the jealousy coming from Cameron, even though that was a non-issue. She patted him on the hand, cold skin on cold skin, pulling his attention back to her.

"Oh, I'm sure they're scumbags, but their money is green. After the cops found our *friend*, business slowed a little."

As if on cue, Cameron's stomach growled. The thought of food was enough to remind him he needed to feed.

Out of the predator lurking in him and pure curiosity, Cameron turned back to look at the two men. They no longer gazed at Sarin but had their heads close in a conspiratory conversation. Cameron focused, willing his hearing to their whispers.

"...on the forum?" Mustache asked Acne.

Acne played with the condensation on the side of his cup. "I heard the chatter, but didn't know if it was legit."

Mustache smiled—the four hairs on his lip twitched. "Oh, it's legit. I even drove by L-Mart earlier to look. The camper is tucked away out back, just on the edge of the property."

Acne looked stunned and grinned. "Really? Some legit cheese pizza?"

Mustache nodded. "Yup, legit and fresh, or so I've heard. Come on, man, you need to be more up on the forum." He drank and smacked his lips together. "You want to grab a slice later?"

Acne nodded, "Absolutely. Ever since joining the forum, I've wanted a taste."

"Well, my friend, tonight is the night." Mustache held up his glass in a toast.

Cameron turned, ignoring the rest of their disgusting conversation.

"What?" Sarin asked. "What is it?" She could see the disturbed look on his face.

He moved in close to her, not that anyone was within earshot. "I think I know where we can feed tonight."

Sarin perked up. She was just as hungry, even though she didn't show it.

"Really? I'm certainly intrigued."

He looked back at the two guys, who were laughing. The urge to change, to show them his true form, to rip them apart and feed on their gore, was nearly painful. With every kill, he had a bit of human remorse, sometimes before the blood was even spilled. Sarin promised it would go away, but he didn't think that was happening after two years. Not these two. No, if Cameron had the chance to kill them, to make them suffer, he would. But, he knew there was someone else more deserving of his wrath. Blood would be shed that night, for that he was sure.

"Do you know what 'cheese pizza' is?" he asked Sarin.

She furrowed her brows like it was a stupid question. "Ah, yes. It's a round, baked meal with sauce and...cheese."

Sarin had been a vampire for hundreds of years, but for once, Cameron felt like he knew something she didn't.

"Well, yes, but that's not what these guys are talking about."

Sarin was confused but trusted Cameron.

He checked the time. "In a few hours, it'll all make sense." The sound of glass shattering grabbed their attention.

"God dammit," Sarin said, throwing her hands in the air. "Fucking Mickey broke another glass." She turned to walk away.

"I guess you never ordered the plastic ones?" Cameron remarked.

Sarin stopped and gave him the middle finger, but with a smile.

He smiled, too, knowing he would be full of delicious, nurturing blood in just a few hours.

ERIC SAT AT THE SMALL TABLE IN THE CAMPER. HE WATCHED football on a fuzzy, black-and-white TV and drank a beer. He tipped the beer back, draining it, and burped.

"Charlotte, get daddy another beer, would'ya?" He asked his 7-year-old daughter.

Charlotte was lying on the camper's floor with a coloring book in front of her. She had a pink crayon clutched in her hand and was putting the finishing touches on a mouse picture. She set her crayon down, got up and grabbed her father a beer.

"Here, Daddy," she said, handing him the cold can.

"Thank ya, darlin." Eric grabbed it without looking and opened it. He took a long pull, his eyes still on the TV. He didn't look at Charlotte much—not since they'd begun their road trip and his little side business. After the first time, the first stop, he'd wept, but not as much as Charlotte. Since then, it had gotten more manageable for him, but not for her. It mattered little. Money needed to be made, and every family member had to pull their weight. It just so happened that he didn't have a job; it was just the two of them.

Once Eric mastered the internet and found the proper forums, things got better. Much easier and much more money. There were undoubtedly some sick fucks in the world.

The flash of headlights and the sound of gravel under tires made both of them look up. A car door closed and they could hear the approaching footsteps.

Eric smiled as knuckles gently knocked on the thin door. He got up and looked down at Charlotte, who was standing. She had a light mist of tears in her eyes already. Her lower lip quivered, knowing what was about to happen.

Eric opened the door and saw a young man standing there. He was a big kid with a reddish beard and hard eyes, who looked at Eric like he was mad, but it was probably fear. This kid was a first-timer to the world of cheese pizza and Eric knew he was about to get paid.

"Can I come in?" the big kid asked.

Eric smiled. His teeth were wide and tobacco-stained. He stepped back and gestured for the guy to enter.

"Please, come on in and make yourself comfortable, friend."

The man smiled, but the look of anger didn't fade.

CAMERON WALKED INTO THE TIGHT CAMPER, FEELING IT ROCK UNDER his weight. It stunk. It had the smells of unwashed flesh, beer, and fear. The man, whose name he could not care less about, grabbed a can of beer from a small table. He sipped it and smiled.

"Ah," the man said, smacking his lips together. "That there is Charlotte." He pointed with the can still in his hand.

Cameron looked at the girl. She couldn't have been over seven and was fighting back tears.

"H-hi," she stammered, looking at the floor. She clutched a coloring book to her chest.

"Okay, darlin, go in the room and get ready. Daddy and this man have grown-up stuff to discuss. He'll be in soon." The man smiled at his daughter and then back to Cameron.

Cameron was a fucking tempest. The storm in his body was raging and his black heart felt like it was going to explode. His fangs were begging—no, screaming—to come out, to rip this piece of human garbage to shreds.

Charlotte nodded, but didn't speak. Instead, she turned and entered a small room, closing the door behind her.

"So," the man started, "it's $100 for a half hour and $150 for an hour." He was looking at Cameron. "Anything goes." The man winked.

It was time, fucking glorious time. Cameron had been waiting since he heard the two losers at the club. He wished those two cunts would show up as well. They would die, not even for food, but just to rid the world of their evil.

"Hey, partner, you okay?" the man asked, noticing a subtle shift in Cameron's face.

Cameron was more than okay; he was excited and *hungry*. He relaxed and allowed his true form to come out. His bones shifted, making room for the rows of teeth. The tips of his fingers hardened into claws, perfect for shredding flesh, digging deep to find hidden blood.

The man opened his mouth to scream, but Cameron wasn't about to let that happen. With a burst of unnatural speed, Cameron reached into the man's mouth and grabbed his lower jaw.

Tears streamed down the man's face and his pathetic human hands pulled at Cameron's, which might as well have been constructed of steel.

Cameron's clawed fingers pinned the man's tongue to the bottom of his mouth. He smiled…and twisted.

The man's jaw popped from the joint with a crack, but Cameron was far from done.

Cameron pulled the man closer, yanking him by his destroyed mouth. He thrashed, hearing more bone and tendons fall to his wrath. Cameron's claws pierced the man's tongue and stretched to the max. The muscle began tearing at the base and oozing blood. Delicious blood.

The man was gagging on his gore. He coughed a mist of crimson into Cameron's face; just a taste of what was to come. Cameron licked it, stretching his tongue to get every drop. Then, with a final pull, the man's jaw came free. His tongue was reduced to a ragged root of bloody, pink flesh. The man fell to the floor and Cameron followed.

His bloodlust was uncontrollable. As much as he wanted to make the man suffer, every spilled drop was one he couldn't enjoy. That couldn't nourish his undead body. He stretched his jaw to the max, closed it over the front of the man's neck, and bit. The veins and arteries erupted, as did the man's dying breath. A beautiful fountain of blood pumped into Cameron's mouth. He drank greedily.

The camper door opened and Sarin watched her creation feed. She didn't mind sharing a kill, especially if she didn't have to do any of the work. Sarin shut the door behind her, her body shifting.

The camper was tight, but she moved in next to Cameron and tore into the man's femoral artery. There wasn't much, but more than enough to quell her hunger.

Cameron relented with one last hard bite, knowing the meal was over. He looked up at Sarin, who was drenched in crimson. His tongue gently sucked at his fangs, tasting every morsel of blood and flesh left by the man.

Sarin stared at Cameron and then glanced over his shoulder.

The bedroom door was opening.

"Daddy?" Charlotte asked, looking at the mangled remains of her father. Her brain wasn't firing right. It took her a moment to realize there were blood-soaked monsters over her father's corpse. When her eyes met Cameron's, she screamed.

"Shh," Cameron pleaded, putting a hellish finger to his lips. He focused and willed his features back to normal, but there was nothing he could do for the blood covering his face. "Shh, please don't cry." Cameron crouched down to her level.

Charlotte clutched a stuffed animal to her chest but didn't move. Instead, her eyes went to Cameron's face and her father's dead body.

"He can't hurt you anymore, I promise," he said, trying to smile. The dried blood on his cheeks cracked.

Charlotte kept looking over his shoulder with fear in her eyes.

Cameron turned and saw Sarin. The other vampire stood there, dripping blood and full of fangs.

"Change back; you're scaring her," Cameron said, trying to keep his voice low, knowing Sarin could hear him just fine.

Sarin didn't move or answer; she just kept staring at the little girl. Her gaze broke from the angelic eyes of Charlotte and back to Cameron.

"Kill her," Sarin ordered.

Cameron looked at her, stunned. "Excuse me? This is a child." He pointed back at Charlotte with his thumb.

Sarin grinned, but there was no humor in her eyes. "No, she's food. She's full of blood, blood which we need to survive. And the blood of the young…" Sarin didn't finish but let her long tongue slither out of her mouth. She smiled and this time, it was genuine.

Cameron was standing now. He faced Sarin, but towered over her, looking down on the more petite vampire. He trembled, but remained in his human form.

"No, we can't. I can't," he stammered. Again, he looked at Sarin's face for any chink in her armor. Something to signify she was lying about killing the girl.

"Yes, you can and will. Or I will." Sarin stepped in closer. "She's seen us, what we are, and what we did. The local police won't believe her, but others will. They almost caught me once and I'm not letting that happen again."

Cameron felt the sting of tears. He took a deep breath and licked his lips, still tasting the blood of the dead man on the floor.

"No, I won't fucking do it." Cameron held his head high in defiance.

Sarin shook her head and sighed. "Fine, I will."

Cameron felt her shift, and she moved in the blink of an eye. He spun and reached out, but it was too late.

Sarin, using only one clawed finger, slit the girl's throat.

Hot blood ran down Charlotte's neck, soaking her shirt. She gasped, like a fish out of water, and collapsed.

"What have you done?" Cameron yelled. The girl's lifeblood pumped from her—her youthful, delicious, reviving blood. He could taste it in the air, the freshness and cleanliness of it. It was different, better than any adult's, and he hadn't even had it in his mouth yet. He was changing, not by his own volition, but by pure nature.

"She's already dead. Don't let her sacrifice be for nothing. Feed, like you were born to do."

Cameron's instinct took over and his body changed. His long tongue ached for the sweet blood soaking into the filthy carpet. With tears in his eyes, Cameron fell to the floor and fed.

Sarin changed back and left the camper. Outside the door, she could hear the ripping of flesh, gulping of blood, and crying.

6

HERE TO KILL

JOHN READ the article and reread it. Then, just to be sure, he read it a third time. A father and daughter, Eric and Charlotte Carmody had been viciously murdered in their camper. This coming after the body of Reggie had been discovered in a dumpster only days earlier. The killings weren't that close, but more than close enough to raise eyebrows.

John didn't need any police or forensics to confirm his suspicions; he knew *what* was killing those people.

He huffed and closed the laptop. That was enough murder for the day, and hopefully, there would be some more soon. John grabbed his cell phone and checked the time. Salim's flight was due to arrive the night before, but an unexpected Atlantic storm had them rerouted to Keflavik airport in Iceland. They were airborne again and should be in the US before lunchtime.

John was a man of patience, but when he knew his goal was in sight, his patience wore thin. Then, with the murder of the little girl and her father, he knew the vampires were becoming more brazen. This brought with it another set of problems altogether. If people, ordinary people, started getting suspicious, or the cops began digging deeper, they'd disappear. That couldn't happen. It had taken

John far too long to track them down; this time, he would see them die in the sun.

His phone dinged with an email. It was Salim.

John read it aloud. "On schedule again. The team is ready and excited."

Simple, and to the point, but it made John's heart race. This was finally going to happen. Finally, the devils that killed his son, using him like an animal to feed on, would die. He'd have his vengeance.

THE PLANE TOUCHED DOWN ON A BACK RUNWAY AT STEWART International Airport in Newburgh, New York. It taxied across the tarmac and the engines were shut down. When it was safe, a pushback was hooked up to the plane. The odd little vehicle pulled the jet, towing it into a private, enclosed hangar.

"Damn, this is fancy as fuck," Mary said, looking out the window as the hangar doors closed.

A sleek Cadillac Escalade, which looked like it had just driven off the showroom floor, sat silent as the pushback came to a halt. Finally, after hours of delays and air travel, the vampire hunters could get off the plane.

Salim grabbed his bag and looked as his crew did the same. "Okay, we're here, but still have work to do." There was a metallic *clang* sound as the staircase was attached to the exit door. He heard footsteps walking up and the door opened.

"John sent me," the man said. He didn't offer a name, but he looked like a bulldog. "Follow me," he said, walking back down the steps.

"Mr. fucking personality," Arthur grumbled, lugging his backpack over his shoulder. He was not in the mood for attitudes, especially from spoiled Americans.

Salim looked at him, stopping him with his glare. He knew Arthur could fly off the handle and had seen it himself. His aggression and *no fucks given* attitude were the main reason he was an ideal vampire killer.

"This is a job," Salim said, looking at all of them in turn. "This is a life-changing opportunity, so act like fucking professionals." He stopped and looked at Arthur, catching the man's gaze. Slowly, Arthur lowered his eyes.

"Yeah, you're right, but still..." he didn't finish, letting it hang in the air.

Salim didn't answer him or look back. Instead, he walked to the top of the stairs and left the plane.

The driver John had sent stood by the massive SUV. The doors were open and Salim could see the smooth, black leather interior. He walked back and set his bag in the cargo space before going to the driver.

"So, where are you taking us?"

The driver looked at him like he was stupid but finally spoke. "John has a house set up, where he'll be greeting you all later tonight. It's not far from here, but we need to get going. You know that patience isn't one of his many virtues as well as I do. Especially when there's something he's passionate about. And this job, this job is top on his list."

The rest of Salim's crew tossed their bags into the SUV and got in. Arthur took up the back row, promptly putting in a pair of wireless earbuds.

"Okay, let's get going then. The sooner we finish, the sooner we get paid," Salim said.

"I don't envy you," the driver said, sliding behind the wheel.

Salim walked around and took the front seat. "Oh no, why is that?"

The enormous engine roared to life with a growl, like a predator. "I've been with John for a few years now. I've seen his business savvy and wealth grow, but this is different. This isn't about money —it's about revenge. It's about righting a wrong and he's put his faith in you." He was looking at Salim, slightly nodding his head. "I wasn't much of a believer until he showed me the truth. Now, I can't look away. And frankly, I don't know what would possess you to do this."

Salim didn't speak and neither did any of his crew. He let the question roll around his brain, but in the end, he didn't have an answer.

SALIM WAS NODDING OFF AFTER THE LONG DRIVE, BUT WHEN HE FELT the large SUV crunch over gravel, he perked up. The driveway was long and winding, full of crushed stone and flanked by a dark tree line. In the distance, he could see the house's silhouette against the purple skyline. A light, a single light, was on, like a beacon calling to them.

"Are we here?" Mary asked. The sound of sleep was thick in her voice.

"Seems that way," Paolo replied from next to her. He stretched and yawned, still feeling the effects of the long drive and flight.

"Looks like John arrived early," the driver said, checking the time on the dashboard.

Salim adjusted in his seat, feeling the tension in his back. "I didn't think he was coming until tomorrow?"

"He wasn't supposed to, but the man isn't the most patient person, especially recently."

The Cadillac pulled up next to a Range Rover and stopped. Sensor lights lit up the driveway and John stood in the doorway.

"Right on time, Charlie," John said, putting a joint to his lips. He took a drag on the potent weed, breathing out the cloud of noxious smoke. He flicked the rest onto the gravel, not bothering to stomp it out. "Please, come inside, come inside."

The vampire hunters grabbed their luggage from the SUV and followed John.

"Is the rest of our stuff and equipment here?" Mary asked Salim. She slung a duffle over her shoulder. "I only have a change of clothes in here." She patted the bag. "The rest of my stuff was on the plane."

Salim didn't know the answer but hoped they'd find out soon. He also needed something fresh to wear. Not to mention, their equipment was on the plane as well. Without it, there was no use in them being there.

John left the door to the house open and they followed him inside. The mudroom was small but led to a large kitchen.

Salim walked into the room, smelling the staleness of the house. This wasn't a house that was used to people; he could tell that right away. John sat at the kitchen island, which had a spread of sandwiches and drinks.

"Please, make yourselves at home," he said, waiting for the last of them to enter.

Salim heard tires on gravel and knew their ride was gone. So this was it; they were there and had a job to do.

Paolo wasted no time with the food. He grabbed a paper plate and two large pieces of the sandwich. Lettuce spilled from the sides when he bit into it. He chewed and nodded in approval before taking another.

"Where's our stuff?" Mary asked, looking around as if their luggage and tools would be in the kitchen.

John looked at her, clearly stoned and smiled. "Everything will be here in the morning. Tonight is a planning and restful night. Tomorrow night, that's when the fun begins."

Salim pulled out a stool and grabbed a bottle of water. He sipped from it and set it down, looking at John.

"So, tomorrow night, huh?"

John picked at a plate of salad, but ate nothing. "Yes. I would've had you out tonight if not for the minor delay. The sooner they're dead, the better."

The sooner we get paid and get home, the better. Salim thought.

"Okay, what's the plan?" Salim asked. His team settled around the island, each with a plate of food.

John walked over to the table, where his laptop was open. "Join me and I'll show you."

John showed them what he'd collected over the years for the next twenty minutes. The news stories, the autopsies, the failed attempt on the vampires with the Visser brothers and, of course, the newest murders.

The hunters were silent. They were pros and knew what they were up against. Each of them formed plans in their heads, thinking of how they'd like to approach the monsters. They knew one fuck up could be their lives. They would be ripped apart mercilessly by the fiends, and their blood would be an unholy meal.

John had finished his presentation, something he'd been rehearsing for days. It felt good, it felt right, and he was ready. He was prepared to finish this, to avenge his son and those innocents killed by the unholy beasts.

"I want them alive," he said.

All the hunters looked at him and then at Salim, who sat staring.

"I want them alive and brought here. I want to watch them die in the sunlight. To burn and melt, turning into slag heaps of corrupted flesh. I want to see the fear on their faces, knowing I did this to them. That is what I want. No, that's what I demand."

Mary leaned in close to Salim and whispered. "Are we going to do this?"

He silenced her with a glance. When John first called Salim, he told him he wanted to watch them die in the sunlight. He should've known the man was serious.

"Consider it done," Salim said. The rest of them didn't speak. It wasn't an impossible job, but capturing was much more dangerous. Salim didn't have a choice. They were already there and had received half of the pay.

Arthur opened his mouth to speak, but shut it. For once, he used his brain before speaking.

"Your equipment will be here in the morning, but I took the liberty of ordering you some updated tools. I think you'll be pleasantly surprised with what you have." John stood and checked the time. "I'm heading off to bed, but don't let me stop you from having fun." He waved at the food and drinks. "The fridge is stocked, and there's more liquor if you'd like."

Mary perked up at that but kept her mouth shut. She dry-washed her hands under the table; the urge to wrap them around a glass of booze was almost too much.

"The bedrooms upstairs are made up for you, so go wherever you'd like." He stifled a yawn with the back of his hand. "I'll see you in the morning." John walked away, his footsteps echoing through the house.

"We're not really going to capture these fucks, are we?" Arthur asked. He leaned in close, like it was a conspiracy.

"Yeah, Salim, you know that's some risky business," Paolo chimed in. A few crumbs sat on his chin.

Salim looked at each of them. The people were there because they were the best. They'd each been in situations similar or worse and had come out on top. They'd also dealt with European vampires, the original vampires—vampires that had been alive for centuries. These Americans were babies compared to their prede-cessors. Capturing them shouldn't be an issue, at least he hoped.

"We catch them, bring them here and let John watch them burn. Then we fly home loaded and set for the rest of our lives. How does that sound?"

They each looked around and nodded. Then, when Salim reminded them of the money, the final score to set them up for life, the thought of capture didn't sound so far-fetched.

"Okay, we'll grab these fucks," Arthur said, standing up and walking over to the island. "But tonight, I'm getting drunk," he said, holding a bottle of bourbon.

Salim smiled. "Pour me some, fuck it. You only live once." He reached out to take the plastic cup.

Unless you're a vampire, he thought, sipping the harsh liquor.

7

THE LAST CALL

CAMERON MILLED ABOUT THE CLUB, keeping busy with the growing crowd. Whether it was helping at the bar or running drinks, it didn't matter. He just needed to stay active and stay away from Sarin.

It had been two nights since he'd fed on the blood of young Charlotte. Even though it was a few towns over, the gruesome murders still made headlines. What made it worse was when the police discovered what a monster her father had been, some viewed her death as a blessing, but they were a silent minority.

Sarin was one of those minorities. She wouldn't hear any differently, regardless of what Cameron said. The rest of the population who sided with her felt that way because of the abuse, but Sarin's thoughts were more nefarious. The little girl couldn't see them for what they truly were and live. It couldn't happen.

Still, it had been difficult for Cameron to cope with. In his old life, in the shit-hole apartment he'd shared with his alcoholic prostitute of a mother, there had been plenty of young kids who lived at the complex. One girl, Shannon, was his neighbor for only a year.

Shannon was the kind of kid he wanted as a little sister. She was always happy and bubbly, despite the growing bruises on her arms and occasionally, her face. She claimed to be the clumsiest kid, but Cameron wasn't stupid. Especially growing up the way he did. He never told Shannon he knew about the abuse, but deep down, they had a connection. And then, one day, they were gone. Her, her three siblings and her parents, gone, like a puff of smoke. They'd left quite a bit of their meager belongings behind but were gone in the night. He often thought of her and what had happened. He knew now that if he found her, it would be different. Somehow, it would be different.

When he watched Charlotte gasping for air as blood poured from her slit throat, he saw Shannon. Saw the fear of an abused child who thought there would be salvation for a second. But, no, the world is cruel and full of monsters; he was now one of them.

Cameron lifted a tray of drinks, using his uncanny balance not to spill a drop. He glided through the crowd, avoiding dancing bodies, and delivered the drinks. He tucked the tray under his arm with a small flourish and returned to the bar. He glanced up at the balcony, catching the predatory glare of Sarin looking down at him. Before he could look away, she smiled.

It had been two years since he'd been reborn a vampire and fucked her countless times, but still, that smile made his black heart quiver. Cameron set the tray on the bar.

"Okay, are you all caught up?" he asked Mickey.

"Sure thing, thank you," Mickey said with the soda gun in one hand and a bottle of vodka in the other. He stuffed two red stirrers in each drink and handed them to waiting customers.

Cameron nodded, letting his bartender work. He scanned the room, looking for anything to do, but his employees were on top of it. Cameron glanced back up at Sarin, whose eyes were still locked on him. He felt like a field mouse under the gaze of an eagle. Again, she smiled, this time showing teeth, and gave him a slight head nod. He smiled back, a natural reaction when a gorgeous creature smiled at you. As if on autopilot, Cameron started walking toward the steps leading to the balcony.

"Pretty big crowd," Sarin said, as Cameron slid next to her at the railing.

Cameron looked down at the milling bodies. The thump of the music vibrated the air, giving life to the crowd like an electric heartbeat. Sarin's smell, the faint hint of apples, drove him wild.

"Yeah, it's a good night." He turned to face her, shocked to find her only inches from him.

Her lips, her cold, undead lips, pressed against his, her tongue slithering into his mouth.

Cameron yielded, opening his mouth to accept her gift of lust. He could feel his cock stiffen at her kiss and knew everything would be alright.

JOHN WATCHED THE VAMPIRES KISS IN DISGUST. HE STOOD AT THE entrance, waiting for the rest of his hired killers to make their way through security. Security was a loose word for what stood at the door. It was only a few thugs with lights checking IDs, no pat downs or metal detectors, which he knew in advance.

He stilled his hand and tongue, which wanted to point and scream, calling out the vile beasts. His patience was thin, but he knew the end was near. After a calming breath, he settled himself down, knowing their reign of terror was coming to an end—an end of purifying sunlight and death.

"Not bad, not bad at all," Arthur said, moving up near John. His eyes wandered to the bodies of young women walking by. He gave them a wink, but only received laughs in return. "Hey, fuck you too," he said, but they were out of earshot.

Paolo laughed, "My friend, these kids could be *our* kids." He put a hand on Arthur's shoulder. "Unless they brought their mothers, your hand will be the only thing you fuck tonight."

"No one is fucking tonight," Salim said, walking up next to them with Mary in tow. His dark eyes looked at each of them, stilling them like children. "This is a fucking job, not a vacation," he lowered his voice. "Don't forget why we're here, or you'll die and die horribly."

Arthur and Paolo looked down at their shoes, knowing they were in the wrong.

"It was just a joke," Arthur said.

"Get your fucking heads in the game," Salim whispered, getting closer to the man.

Arthur nodded.

John watched the exchange with a smile. He knew this time would be different. The vampires would die for the last time and he'd watch them burn. Part of him wanted the vampire hunters to kill the beasts quickly. He knew they had their ways, especially with fire. But, he wasn't paying millions for a quick death. No, this was personal and he wanted them to feel fear, if that was still possible. John needed them to know it was him that killed them, to avenge his boy.

The plan was a simple one, but often simple is better. There was no better way to catch a predator than with bait. Predators can't resist the taste of blood, whether it's coyotes, bear, fox or vampires. The prospect of an easy meal, especially when hungry, would drive them forward right into the trap's jaws.

John was excited, but tense. He needed something to take the edge off, but was worried about smoking weed. The last thing he needed was to step outside for a toke and have the security guard not let him back in. That would put a fucking damper on his plans. A drink, but only one, would probably do the trick. It would also allow him to move around a little and blend in. He was the only one in the club over sixty, so it wasn't easy for him to mix. He'd dressed the part, though. Tighter clothes, flashier material. He'd even discovered his old ear piercing was still open enough for him to get a gold hoop into. It stung, but was worth it. He looked like he was hunting a young woman or man, not vampires.

The bartender tossed drinks on the bar, sloshing a bit onto the wooden top. He turned when finished with the customers and looked at John. "What can I getcha?"

John looked at the liquor bottles behind the bar. "Um, how about an old-fashioned with the top shelf?"

The bartender nodded and began working on the drink.

John wanted to talk to him, make small talk, and learn about the vampires, but he was certain the bartender would have no idea. At least he hoped he didn't. He could feel their glare on him, like it was physical. Like their undead fingers were scratching at his back, burrowing into his flesh. Casually, he turned around and leaned against the bar, his eyes playing up towards the balcony. They were still there, looking down on the unsuspecting people. Like this was an abattoir and they were the fucking butchers. Their knives were sharpened and ready to slit throats. Little did they know what was in store for them.

Salim saw John at the bar and gave a slight nod. It wasn't one of encouragement but said, *be careful.*

"Here ya go," the bartender said to John's back.

John turned around and faced the young man. He didn't ask for a price and didn't care. Instead, he tossed a twenty on the bar and stirred his drink.

The bartender took the money and went to make change.

"Keep it," John said, taking his first sip. It was strong, so he'd have to go slow.

"Oh, thank you," the bartender said with a smile.

No one else had bellied up to the bar, and John felt ambitious. His curiosity and the spreading warmth of liquor in his belly forced his hand. "So, what's going on up there?" he asked, gesturing to the balcony. "Private party or something?" He sipped from his glass, watching the bartender's eyes glance up.

"Oh no, that's open for everyone. Most people hang out down here, but there's another bar and some tables up there. Those two," he pointed to the vampires at the railing, "they're the owners."

John nodded, hoping his expression was normal, considering his heart was racing.

"Sarin and Cameron," he said, picking up a glass to clean.

"They're pretty young, but have a great business sense. Plus, they're good to us."

John wanted to scream in his face. Tell this young fuck that his bosses were undead killers, who would feed on him the second they could.

A customer came up to the bar, stealing the bartender's attention, but John was done anyway. He needed to walk away before he said something that would blow the operation. He knew the vampires could probably hear him talk, even from that distance and the last thing he wanted to do was tip their hand. He sipped his drink and rejoined his group. His eyes flicked back to the balcony, but the vampires were gone.

THE OFFICE WASN'T HUGE, BUT VAMPIRES WEREN'T BOTHERED WITH cramped spaces. Sarin sat on the desk and Cameron in the chair in front of her. He had his head down like a child in the principal's office.

Sarin didn't rush him. She knew what he was dealing with; she'd been there too. All vampires had that feeling, that *human* feeling, for particular kills. Maybe their food reminded them of a family member, or they had problems eating children or women. Each had their own set of issues, but they could all be worked out in time. Time was one thing they had plenty of.

Cameron lifted his head and fixed his hair. At least he hoped he fixed it. The lack of mirrors made certain vanity things an issue, but he didn't really care. He knew he looked good and for the first time in his life, he was confident. He gazed up at Sarin, and the look she was giving him, lustful and hungry, was all the reassurance he needed.

The thought of the little girl kept racing around his brain, nagging him. He knew Sarin was right, that he needed to feed, but he still felt wrong. In his black heart, he enjoyed the kill. The taste of her innocent, sweet, refreshing blood made him shiver with memory. No, he wasn't ashamed of drinking her blood, but the fact he wanted more. In his mind, adult blood was dull and mundane, but a child's blood was divine. It was the difference between roadkill and a filet mignon. Cameron salivated at the thought.

Sarin took her eyes off him and looked up at the TV on the wall. It was split into multiple cameras of the club. It was running smoothly; the perfect cover and lucrative money maker for them. She scanned the screens, not concerned about the employees, but a specific group that had come in. There wasn't anything over-whelming about them. Certainly not enough to cause alarm, but they'd caught her eye—the old man in particular. The Black Heart saw its fair share of customers and the occasional senior citizen wasn't out of the ordinary. But this one guy had been staring a little too hard at them. That, again wasn't odd, considering Sarin had been wearing a snug, black shirt that exposed more than a little of her supple breasts. The man didn't look at her in lust but almost disgust. He sat with a group of younger men and a woman, each with drinks. Their heads were close in conversation, which was needed over the loud music. They all raised a toast, touched their glasses and downed their drinks.

Sarin pushed them from her mind and slid off the desk. She crouched down in front of Cameron, looking him in the eyes.

"Look, I know you're not happy with me, and that's fine." She put her hand to her chest. "But, just remember what you are. Remember how you survive. You are no longer a human, Cameron. You're a vampire, and vampires feed off the living. And sometimes, the best *food* is a meal we never would've considered in our former lives."

Sarin looked away from him for a moment. Images of her former life, her early life as a vampire, flashed in her brain. The dead bodies, the ripped open throats, the fear masks and the smile across her creator's face, Marcellus.

Cameron watched her, drinking her in. Her beauty was almost blinding and her scent drove him wild. Their sexual appetite was nearly as voracious as their lust for death and blood. They hadn't fucked since the death of Charlotte in the trailer and Cameron was feeling it. As mad as he was over the last few days, he still wanted her. Being close to her, seeing her breasts peeking out of her shirt, staring at those lips. He was stiffening. Sex aside, he knew she was right. They were predators, plain and simple. As a human, he didn't weep when he ate meat. Hell, he didn't even know what half of it was, nor what age the animal was. This was no different. It was just going to take time.

"When I was born," she said, looking back at him, "my creator, Marcellus, went through the same thing with me. I didn't know what was wrong with me. I was starving yet repulsed at the same time. My first taste of blood, my first *true* taste, when I let myself relax and instinct take over…" She trailed off, looking up at the ceiling, with a slight grin. "Well, needless to say, I was over my apprehension rather quickly. Marcellus made sure of that." She looked back at Cameron, a stern look replacing the smile. "If you think what I did in the trailer was bad," she waved a hand, dismissing the thought. "Marcellus, he was a killer, a taker of lives, an old vampire and a vicious one."

Cameron was listening, but with a twinge of jealousy. He had no reason to be jealous, but he was. It was like hearing about an old boyfriend and the sex they'd had. He shook the notion from his head.

"And what happened to him?"

Sarin looked at Cameron, but didn't *see* him. It was like he was a ghost and she was staring through him. "I left," she said. "We had a…" Sarin licked her lips and sucked at her teeth, "a rather nasty disagreement and I knew it was time to move on."

Cameron watched a flash of emotions dance over her face. He reached out gently and took her chin in his hand. "This," he said, looking around the room, "has been the greatest gift anyone could've given me." He brought his eyes back to hers, which were misty. "And I have you to thank for it." Cameron felt his black heart quiver at the faint smile that bloomed on Sarin's face. He leaned in and kissed her.

Sarin breathed into his mouth, a sigh of relief, mixed with lust.

Her tongue bullied its way past his lips and tasted him. She stood, making his head rise with hers. Their lips never came apart.

Cameron's hands rose, blindly searching her chest, cupping her breasts. He began unbuttoning her shirt but grew impatient. With both hands, he ripped her shirt open, revealing her chest. Her tits were covered in black lace, and he knew *if* she wore panties, they'd match.

Sarin's hands went behind her back and unclasped the bra, before Cameron could tear it from her. It was one of her favorites.

The undergarment came away in his hands and he threw it across the room. His mouth, his hungry mouth, descended on her taut nipples.

Sarin gasped as he pulled one of the cherry nubs into his mouth, biting it gently. She needed him badly. It was her turn to fumble around. She reached down and found his cock begging to be released. A thin coating of pre-cum made the outside of his pants slick and she knew they'd both need a change of clothes. She unsnapped his pants and dove inside.

Cameron did his best to wiggle, allowing his manhood to be freed. Finally, with Sarin guiding him, his cock popped out, standing at attention.

Sarin pushed his head away from her chest and fell to her knees. Without warning, she took him in her mouth.

"Oh, fuck!" Cameron muttered as Sarin licked his shaft. Her tongue played over his helmet and her eyes came up to meet his. She had a beautiful, seductive smile on her face. Cameron knew he'd follow her to the ends of the earth.

"I just needed a quick taste," she said, standing up and pulling her tight pants off.

Cameron was right—she was wearing a black lace thong—which she left on.

Sarin kicked her pants away and mounted Cameron in the chair. She pulled her panties to the side, revealing her hungry, cold pussy. She impaled herself with him, taking his penis to the base.

THE LAST CALL | 81

Cameron's hands guided Sarin's tits back to his mouth, but he had difficulty deciding which to suck.

It didn't matter; her orgasm was coming and coming fast. Within moments, she quivered and bit down into his shoulder. The waves of pleasure squeezed him, and as hers was ebbing away, his was rising.

Cameron unleashed a torrent of cum inside her with a guttural moan and growl.

Sarin looked down at him, their lips touching. Her black hair created a shroud around them as they kissed. They didn't speak, just sat there, joined together.

Cameron wanted to say that he loved her because deep inside him, for the first time, he loved another. When their lips separated, and her eyes opened, he was nearly overcome with emotion. His lips, still tasting of hers, parted. "Sarin, I —,"

"Shh," she whispered, her mouth almost brushing his. "Don't say it." Sarin kissed the corner of his mouth and rested her head on his shoulder. "I know," she breathed into his ear. Her hand found its way to the back of his head, stroking his hair. "Me too."

Cameron wrapped his arms around her like a vice but had no fear of hurting her. He squeezed and felt a burn in his eyes. He never did say it; there was no reason to. In the end, he never would.

JOHN AND THE OTHERS SAT WITH THEIR HEADS CLOSE TOGETHER. Their plan had long been decided, but now it was time. The locations were set, the killers were ready, and John was undoubtedly prepared to watch them die.

He looked away from the group, who were more relaxed than he felt was appropriate. John was electric, like a lightning rod in a storm. He was buzzing and it wasn't from the alcohol. This had to go perfectly, or they'd suffer the same fate as the Visser brothers. He didn't know how, but he could sense the vampires; they were back. John's eyes scanned the crowd and found them.

They had come from a back room and with smiles on their faces. He'd seen that look before but didn't notice it earlier: love. These two monsters were in love with each other and whatever triste they had earlier was over. They smiled and held each other close like it was nothing. Like they hadn't slaughtered a man and his daughter only days earlier. Or the fact they hadn't fucking murdered his son, his baby boy, treating him like nothing but a meal.

John clenched his fists and could feel his vision wavering at the rush of blood to his head and face. He began standing, not knowing what to do next. It didn't matter; he was going to do something. Throw something in their face, shout them out as monsters, or attack them with fists and maybe a knife.

"John, it'll be done," Salim said, his strong hand grabbing John's forearm. His dark eyes had flashed from cheerful to serious, like a traffic light changing from red to green. "Just sit down and relax."

John looked at Salim and knew the man was right. He snapped out of his murderous trance, questioning his sanity for a second. He was an old man with no combat training, or appropriate weapons. The vampires may not have killed him in front of the crowd, but they'd be gone before the sun.

"I'm sorry," John muttered, suddenly embarrassed at his rash decision. "I think I need to smoke a joint or something. Calm my nerves."

Salim looked at his watch. The rest of the table had gone quiet when they'd noticed John trying to get up with a look of death in his eyes.

"I think it's time to go anyway," Salim said, standing up. The club will be closing in the next few hours.

The rest of them stood, not talking. There was no need; they knew their roles in this plan before leaving the house. Now was the fun part; waiting to spring the trap while not dying in the process.

Salim looked at them, each of them. It was only for a moment, but he needed to ensure they were all ready and clear.

They were professionals and had killed before. Salim knew they'd kill again.

"Let's go," he said, not waiting for a response, and walked towards the exit.

AFTER A LONG AND MOSTLY UNEVENTFUL NIGHT, THE BLACK HEART was finally closed. The last light had been turned off, and the parking lot was empty. There was nothing but silence and vampires left behind.

Sarin and Cameron stood outside, looking up at the night sky. Their city wasn't huge, but the lights of humanity could wash out the heavens.

Sarin's mind wandered back to her youth when she'd first met Marcellus. The sky was different then, like every star was a beacon calling her. She thought the sky was bright when she was a girl, but it was nearly blinding in its brilliance when she'd become a vampire. But, time seemed to distort and warp everything.

In the distance, she could hear sirens and car horns blaring, but the sky was quiet—just a patch of darkness with the most minute pin-pricks of light.

Cameron pulled the door closed behind him, checking the lock.

"Shall we?" he asked, offering his arm.

Sarin looped hers into his, feeling the cold of his undead flesh through his clothes.

Together, they walked down the back steps and into the night. Sarin pulled him closer and rested her head on his shoulder. She was an immortal killer, lusting for flesh and blood, yet being close to him did something to her; it gave her hope.

It was a feeling she hadn't felt in decades. Even when she'd been with Vee-Exx, her former lover and bandmate, things hadn't been perfect. Their lives were different; at times, they seemed to coexist out of comfort, rather than true companionship. She'd only been with Cameron for a few years, but still, he was different.

Her mind wandered back to Marcellus and how she'd felt with him. Their time together, traveling the US in the late 1800s and early 1900s had been a whirlwind of murder, feeding, sex and betrayal. It was a time in her life as a vampire that she both cherished and loathed. She'd committed heinous acts with him, things that would stay in her brain until the end. Or until the sun claimed her. She also remembered Marcellus' strength and attitude. He was a man who didn't care, taking what he wanted. It was probably because he was already hundreds of years old and had seen and done it all. There was no compassion in his black heart, only lust and murder. That little girl would've suffered if he had been in the camper earlier. The father would've been slaughtered, and he would've played with her, drawing out her torture. That was his thing with children; he said they tasted better after a round of pain. Still, Sarin hoped Cameron had rid himself of the human compassion he once possessed. It was a thing of the past and hesitation now could get them discovered and hunted. Part of her loved him for the fact he was still so innocent, but another part of her cringed at it.

Cameron had been a vampire for a few years. Sarin had hoped that part of him was gone, as it usually was for most of them after a few months. However, his caring heart remained, at least part of it.

"It's beautiful out, isn't it?" Cameron spoke, snapping Sarin out of her reverie.

She looked up at him, the heavens reflecting in her eyes. She smiled, showing a glint of her teeth—her perfectly normal, human teeth.

"Hmm, it is," she said, slowing him down to kiss him. It wasn't a kiss of passion but one of love.

They were alone on the dark street. It was the deep hours of the morning, the time when traffic almost stopped. Like the world was holding its breath, getting ready for another day. A time of blackness and calm. A time of vampires.

"I know we talked about it, but just remember what you felt the other day is normal," Sarin said, gazing up at him.

Cameron gave her a smirk, but he knew deep down inside he should be over it. He should've been over it the first time he'd taken the life of a terrified adult. That first spray of arterial blood coursing into his mouth. The feeling it gave him. The rejuvenation. The satiation of his new found hunger.

"I know, and trust me, I think I'm over it," he said, but deep down, he didn't know if that was the truth.

Sarin kissed him again. "It takes time getting used to this," she waved her hand out into the darkened street. "This life of darkness, of death. We are children of the night and this is our time for all eternity."

Sarin stopped talking as a black dog crossed their path. It froze and looked at them with glowing red eyes. Then, slowly and deliberately, the dog nodded before loping into the shadows.

Sarin smiled. "It seems we're not the only ones out tonight."

A scream, a shrill, pained *human* scream, ripped through the silence of the night.

Their heads snapped, their sharp ears picking up the area of the altercation. Not only was there a shout, but it sounded like a scuffle. At least two people were fighting, one being a woman. Both being food.

"Hungry?" Sarin asked, her smile widening.

Cameron knew this was his chance to show her he'd pushed away his human emotions. He would save this woman, letting her thank her saviors, and then rip her apart.

"Oh, I'm ready." His teeth were shifting, turning to points in his mouth.

"Show me. Show me you're a fucking killer," Sarin moaned, almost sexually. Her teeth were changing as well, shifting bone and flesh.

"I will, oh I fucking will," Cameron said, kissing her hard and deep, their razor-sharp teeth clashing. He felt himself hardening and knew what was to come after they fed.

The sounds of grunting and fist vs. flesh came from the depths of a black alley. Well, it would've been pitch black to the human eye, but to the vampires, it was perfect.

They stood at the mouth of the alley, and Cameron said, "Hey, what the fuck is going on here?"

THE WINDOWS OF JOHN'S CAR WERE FOGGY, BUT HE DIDN'T DARE start it. He figured he was far enough away from the alley, but he couldn't be too careful. He knew what the vampires were capable of and agreed with Salim to keep his distance. Gazing through binoculars would have to do.

His breath fogged the windows as he watched the vampires approach the alley. John started getting dizzy and realized he'd been holding his breath. He let it out, creating more fog on the window. He adjusted in the driver's seat, pushing the big lenses around the opaque patch.

"Come on, you fucks," he muttered to himself. His heart was trying to escape his ribcage. Every thump could be felt in his temples, thudding into his brain. His mouth was dry and his armpits were soaked with anticipation.

"Get in the fucking alley," he said, careful not to be too loud. He was far away but knew the vampires' senses were inhuman. He hoped his hunters knew what they were doing. It was dark, and pitch black in the alley, but these were creatures of the night. John didn't know how well they could see in the dark.

The male vampire, who he'd learned was named Cameron, said something. John could just see the side of his mouth in the distance. He couldn't determine what was said, but it didn't matter.

"Come the fuck on," he said, a little louder than he intended. They were still outside of the alley, but something was happening. The female vampire, Sarin, was changing. Her face was shifting and in the shadows of the night, he could see her true form taking shape.

John's throat felt like sandpaper. His testicles pulled tight against his body and were covered in a cold sweat. He lowered the binoculars. "Fuck," he said.

The vampires entered the alley.

THE CARDBOARD UNDER MARY WAS DAMP. IT WAS BETTER THAN LYING on the wet ground, but she knew she'd need to change her clothes later, if she survived. That was no way to think and she pushed the thought from her mind. This wasn't her first time being used as vampire bait, but if it were her last, she wouldn't complain.

When she'd first become a nun, if anyone had told her in only a few years she'd be a notorious vampire slayer, she would've had them committed.

It was dark in the alley, but she could still see Salim standing over her. He'd been punching himself in the hand, keeping it in tune with her screams. The mouth of the alley was slightly brighter, and two forms blotted out some of the light. Salim looked down at her but didn't speak. Mary just nodded, and drew the Glock 17 she'd had in her waistband. The gun sported a long suppressor, which screwed into the barrel. The sound wouldn't be eliminated, but it would help, that was for sure. She'd checked it many times, but had the urge to recheck it. She knew that wasn't possible; the vampires would surely hear that. Gently, she touched the slide, feeling the indicator, letting her know a round was in the chamber.

The gun was a standard Glock 17, but the ammunition was far from ordinary. Each round was blessed, made with holy water from the river Jordan. They all knew the bullets wouldn't kill the vampires, but they would weaken them. Death would come with the sun, a request from John.

"Hey, what the fuck is going on here?" Cameron yelled from the mouth of the alley.

Salim took a deep breath and turned. "What the fuck is it to you?" He looked back towards the mouth of the alley. His gun was also in his waistband, but he didn't draw it. It was too soon.

Paolo and Arthur were crouched low behind a dumpster. They had guns as well, but their role wasn't shooting. Each of them had a length of rope fastened like an old west lasso. Usually, trying to restrain two vampires with ordinary rope would be suicide. Luckily for them, their rope was far from normal. The fibers of this rope were interwoven with strands of silver. Silver was one of the few things that would render a vampire's power almost useless. They hoped it was enough. Paolo and Arthur slowed their breathing, almost holding it so the vampires wouldn't hear them. They held their ropes tight, preparing to spring their traps.

"Well, it seems like something is going on here. Something involving the woman on the ground."

Salim hoped the shock on his face wasn't apparent. The vampires were still quite a ways off and they could already see Mary. He hoped her gun was hidden.

"Fuck you, buddy. And your skank girlfriend," Salim yelled, hoping there wasn't anyone else on the street. "This is none of your business, so fuck off." He wanted to draw them but not attract others. Especially the police.

"Well, now that's not very nice," Cameron said, walking further into the alley. Sarin was at his heels, but her head was down. "And I want to make it my fucking business," Cameron growled.

Salim steeled his nerves and watched as the vampire started to shift.

Cameron was nearing the dumpsters, his eyes locked on Salim. His face was transforming, his teeth growing, his bones shifting. A sinister, hungry smile split his face.

Salim, who'd taken a few steps closer to the vampires, backpedaled. He wanted to look at Mary, but she was a professional —she'd be ready. No matter how many vampires he'd slayed, facing down an immortal killer was always terrifying.

"Now, listen here," Salim said. "Just leave me be and we'll get out of here." He kept his eyes locked on Cameron. His eyes were adjusted to the gloom, more than enough to see the vampire in front of him.

"Oh, friend, it's far too late for that. Now, it is our fucking business."

Salim was preparing to step aside, allowing Mary a clean shot. The vampires were almost at the dumpster.

Come on, you fuckers. Just a few more steps, he thought.

Cameron tensed like a lion on the plains, preparing to launch itself upon a gazelle.

A hand, a claw-tipped hand, grabbed Cameron's arm, stopping him in place.

Salim's heart was pounding—he heard Mary adjust behind him. Something was wrong, very wrong.

Salim reached for his gun.

SARIN WAS HUNGRY. SHE COULD SMELL THEM AND THEIR FEAR—IT WAS delectable. Once her change began, she wasn't stopping it. It felt great, like putting on a comfortable pair of jeans. She walked close to Cameron, letting him take the lead. Allowing him to *show* her he was a killer—a true killer.

The alley was dark, but she didn't want them to see her face. Even in the diminished light, her change was apparent. She didn't want them to see her, not yet. She wanted the attacker to feel secure and strong, like he was in control. And the victim to believe her white knight had arrived to save her. Sarin knew that their emotions would shatter once Cameron entirely shifted, morphing into the killer he truly was.

Sarin stuck close to him, head down, letting her hair cover her face. She salivated with the thought of blood. The smell of the humans was rich in her nose; even the putrescent odor of garbage couldn't obscure the sweetness of their gore.

Cameron traded verbal jabs with the man, moving them deeper into the alley. She followed, her nose pulling her closer to her meal. The scent of human flesh was strong...too strong.

Sarin breathed deeply, focusing on her smell. Her hunger was intense, but her sense of survival, which had kept her alive for hundreds of years, was even more potent.

Ambush! Her mind screamed. There were more people, at least, lying in wait behind the dumpster, which Cameron was nearing. Usually, it wouldn't have mattered. Four humans were just a large meal for two vampires. But, there was something off about this man. The way he spoke, the confidence disguised as confrontation, had Sarin on edge.

Sarin grabbed Cameron's arm, her clawed fingers wrapping around his bicep.

The man's face changed. It wasn't as drastic as the vampires, but it was there. His face flashed with a look of fear and anger—controlled anger. His right hand moved, quick for a human, towards his waistband. As he stepped to the side, a large gun appeared in his hand, revealing the woman on the dirty ground.

The woman also held a gun, raising it at Cameron's chest. The gun spat, much quieter than usual. A flash of light burped from the small hole at the end of the suppressor.

Cameron looked surprised, but wasn't scared. A lead bullet wouldn't do much more than tickle him.

Sarin felt like she was in slow motion. The bullet, followed by many more, ripped into Cameron's undead flesh. Pain and confusion flashed across his hellish face as the bullets tore into him.

Sarin snapped her attention to the man with the gun aimed at her. She'd forgotten about the other two near the dumpster.

The other gun fired. Even with her speed, she couldn't outmaneuver a bullet. Pain, like she'd never experienced, erupted in her body. It was a sharp snap like something hot had broken in her flesh. Her energy dropped with every round that found its mark. And every bullet *did* find its spot.

Sarin tried to turn and run, the thought of a meal no longer on her mind. Survival, that was it. A bullet smashed into her back, the pain nearing untold proportions. She stumbled, nearly tripping over her feet, when something wrapped around her. Something pinned her arms to her side and seemed to vibrate with electricity.

Silver, she thought, trying to fight the restraints. This was it. She'd collapse on the dirty ground and be burned—or left for the sun. Either way, she knew it was her end. The end she thought would've happened in the stream over a hundred years in the past.

Sarin fell to the ground, as weak as a newborn kitten. Her face had changed back; it was too much effort to maintain the vampiric form.

Cameron fell next to her, his face splashing in a puddle of filth. He looked scared and rightfully so. Sarin had dealt with vampire hunters before, but these were a different breed. These were professionals.

She waited for the fire. She anticipated the fire, the dying light of flames, to wash over her. It did not come.

Tires squealed at the mouth of the alley.

"Did you get them? Did you get the fuckers?" An older man yelled.

"Yes, open the fucking hatch and let's get the fuck out of here."

Sarin was fading from consciousness as she was roughly dragged down the alley. She looked up before fading to black.

An older man had a sickening smile plastered on his face. He opened the back lift gate of the massive vehicle.

Sarin was picked up like a sack of flour and thrown into the back of the car. Cameron took three men to put him in, but he was loaded next to her. Dark hoods were thrown over their heads, bathing them in pure darkness.

The other doors opened, and the attackers all piled into the vehicle. With a growl, the car sped away.

Sarin felt weak. The last image she'd seen before the hood was thrown over her head stayed with her: Cameron's terrified face.

8

RED TEETH

John drove like a man on a mission. The night was quiet, even in the populated areas. They flew by a couple of cars, none of which were cops.

"John, you might want to slow down," Salim said from the front passenger seat. He had his suppressed pistol in a shoulder holster concealed by a thin windbreaker. After the quick fight with the vampires, he reloaded, leaving the spent shell casings behind. There was no blood or crime, so it would go unnoticed. Salim knew all DNA evidence burned from a shell casing when fired, so he didn't have to worry about the gun being traced back to him. John would have them destroyed anyway. As soon as the vampires were piles of ash, that is.

John allowed the big V8 to dull to a purr, instead of an all-out roar. He was still sweating, even though the air conditioner was on.

John nodded and said, "You're right, you're right." He hit his directional, leading them further out of the city and towards the house. The last place the vampires would ever see.

"So, what's the plan now?" Mary said from the backseat. She scooted forward to talk with John and Salim.

Arthur and Paolo kept guns trained on the vampires, as if they somehow could break through the silver-lined rope. The knots were tight, but they were experienced hunters and knew their prey. This wasn't over until the vampires were sent to Hell, where they belonged.

"The plan?" John said, not taking his eyes off the road. The city streets gave way to the suburbs, which gave way to the country roads they were now traveling. "The plan is to let the light of the sun burn these fuckers to ash. That, my dear, is the plan." He spat the last word, his heart still racing.

Mary sat back and adjusted her gun. She knew the plan but hoped it had changed. She wanted to torch them in purifying fire, the holy water and gasoline mixture, and be done. Her last night's sleep wasn't the best, and the day's adrenaline was wearing off. The sooner the vampires were dead, the better. She knew one thing, she was getting drunk afterward, Salim be damned.

"Hey, cut the shit," Paolo said, poking Sarin with the barrel of his gun.

"What are they doing back there?" John asked. He looked in the rear-view mirror. The big SUV drifted, but he corrected it before it hit the soft shoulder.

"Eh, nothing much. Just mumbling or something," Arthur said.

A sickening thud of a pistol against flesh sounded in the car, along with a muffled grunt.

"There, that should shut her up," Paolo said. He slid back into his seat, the gun still trained on Sarin.

IT WAS BAD. WORSE THAN ANYTHING SHE'D EVER DEALT WITH. EVEN worse than her birth in the stream. In that case, she thought she might've had a chance. Maybe she could've run from them, or even fought them off. Then, there was a glimmer of hope. Now, there was none. They would burn in the sun and there was nothing they could do about it.

Deep down, Sarin was almost relieved. There is no hiding

anymore. No more running or killing. No more avoiding surveillance cameras or, even worse, mirrors. No, she could finally end it all. Finally, succumb to the sweet embrace of death that should've come for her decades ago. But what about Cameron? He didn't deserve the end he was about to receive. He was a lost boy, a kid really, who drew the short straw at every turn in life. And now he was pulling his final one—which would end in immolation and suffering.

"Cameron," she whispered. Their hearing was terrific, but with the silver sapping their energy, she didn't know how well it would function. She listened through her hood, hoping to get a response. He'd been quiet since they'd been thrown in the vehicle. She could feel the despair oozing from the young vampire. It was defeat—he was defeated, done and surrendered. Since his rebirth, Cameron had known only ultimate power, and it was intoxicating. Now, he lay bound, injured and powerless in the back of a speeding vehicle. A vehicle headed towards certain death for the both of them.

It was faint, but Sarin heard Cameron move. He hissed as he strained against the burning ropes of silver.

"Yes," Cameron moaned. "I'm here."

Sarin smiled. "This is bad; I will not lie," she said, keeping her voice barely audible to the human ear. The road noise would hope-fully drown out the sound. At least, she thought.

"Hey, cut the shit," one of the vampire hunters said. Sarin kept herself from flinching when she felt the muzzle of the gun press against her cold, undead flesh. Guns never scared her, at least ones that fired standard bullets. These guns, with those bullets, now they frightened her. The rounds that were buried in her, throbbed. With every undetectable quiver of her black heart, the bullets burned. They felt like they had a pulse of their own. She didn't know how many there were, but if she escaped this fucking fiasco, she'd need to remove them and fast. If this group could find and capture them, she could only imagine who else was looking for her.

Sarin did as she was told. She couldn't stand the thought of another bullet. The gun smashed into her, but she didn't grunt or respond. She wouldn't give these fucks the pleasure.

Again, she was silent, plotting, thinking of a way to get out of this.

The big SUV continued its trek through the night. The dark, wondrous night, the only saving grace for Sarin and Cameron. But she knew it would end soon. The sun, the arch nemesis of every vampire, would be up soon—then, they'd be ash.

SALIM FOUGHT THE URGE TO GRAB THE HANDLE ABOVE HIS DOOR. THE closer they got to the old house, the faster and wilder John drove. He was an old man, let alone the fact he was excited and thirsting for vengeance. Salim wanted to tell him to slow down, to be careful, but there was no way John would listen again. They were out of the city and into the country now. The only cops working were the county deputies and maybe a trooper. Both were probably in the city looking for a drunk to arrest. Not an older man driving his hundred-thousand-dollar SUV on a back road. They might have had questions if they saw four foreigners, all with unregistered and suppressed handguns. Oh, and the fact they had two vampires tied and subdued in the back of the car.

The SUV took a long, curving turn, the expensive headlights carving up the gloom. It wasn't enough. Salim wouldn't be able to relax until the sun rose. Until then, he was on alert, ready to kill if needed. Fuck the contract and John; if the vampires needed to die early, they died early. He knew the old man would get over it and still pay up. At least, he hoped. Either way, he already had a life-changing amount of money in his account. No, John would pay up, even if things went south and they had to end it fast.

The tires squealed and John jerked the wheel as a turn, one much sharper than anticipated, snuck up on him.

"Fuck, that one came out of nowhere," John said, shaking off the jitters. He let off the gas just a little. "Almost there," he said aloud, but to himself. The house was visible in the distance. They didn't leave many lights on when they'd left, but a few still burned.

"Okay, everyone, show time. Let's look alive, get the targets to their locations and fucking end this," Salim barked, looking back at his team of hired killers.

They all nodded. Paolo and Arthur didn't take their eyes off the vampires—true professionals.

The SUV drove over crushed stone and into the driveway. The house stood silent, with just a few lights on. It didn't matter; soon, the entire thing would be alight. Alight with the glory of the sun. The purifying, cleansing, killing, sun.

John stopped and put the SUV in park. He killed the engine, listening to it tick and cool.

"Paolo, stay gun up until Mary and Arthur can pop the hatch. I'm coming around to support and guide." Salim barked orders like a natural. The chairs, two plain lawn chairs, sat in the driveway, about twenty feet from the house. That was it. Nothing special. Sit them in the chairs and keep guns on them until the sun rises. If they moved, they were to be shot.

Salim hopped out of the SUV, leaving John sitting behind the wheel. He drew his Glock from his shoulder holster and checked to ensure a round was in the chamber. It was. He was no fucking amateur.

Mary and Arthur opened the hatch, guns drawn and ready. They aimed them at the vampires, who were as calm as possible.

Knowing his partners had the vampires covered, Paolo jumped out of the SUV. Salim appeared at his side and they approached the rear of the vehicle.

"Get'em out," Salim said, his gun still drawn.

Mary took a step back, letting Paolo get next to Arthur. Together they dragged Cameron out of the back and let him fall to the ground. Next came Sarin, who found her feet before hitting the earth.

"Get'em in the fucking chairs. I want to take the hoods off'em before the sun rises. I want them to look me in the eyes as they fucking burn." John was out of the car and yelling orders. Spit flew from his mouth as he grimaced at the monsters before him.

SARIN CAUGHT HERSELF BEFORE SHE HIT THE GROUND. SHE GOT HER feet under her, but stumbled forward into waiting arms—rough arms that twisted her around. The hood kept her from seeing whom she'd struck, but it felt and smelled like a man.

Before she was pulled from the SUV, she heard the thump of a body hitting the gravel. There was a whimper, and she knew it was Cameron. She wanted to change, to take the form of a she-devil, of a woman possessed and kill these fuckers. Drink their blood and rip their flesh apart—to kill once again. Something she knew would never happen. Not unless they fucked up. If they did, it would be the end of them. Even weak from the bullets, she would kill and destroy once she was out of the silver-lined rope. She could almost taste their blood: hot, salty, ripe with fear and regret. It was a taste she was familiar with, but one she feared she'd never savor again.

Rough hands grabbed Sarin around the arms and led her forward. She didn't fight, nor speak out. She knew begging was useless. There was no fight left. She would accept the sun with dignity.

Sarin was spun around and pushed hard. She fell, but a plastic chair caught her before she hit the ground.

"Don't fucking move, or I'll put a bullet in you," a male voice said.

Sarin was still. She believed the threat. The multiple bullets in her body proved that these men and women weren't fucking around.

There was a slight struggle she couldn't see, only hear. Another body was dropped hard into a chair next to her.

Cameron, she thought.

The hood was stifling and dark, but she knew it was coming off soon. She knew they wanted to see her face—to see Cameron's face, to watch the fear wash over them as the sky turned pink in the east. When the killing rays of sunlight broke the horizon, seeking the black hearts of the vampires.

JOHN HAD TEARS IN HIS EYES. NOT FROM SADNESS, BUT FROM finality. Finally, the death of his son would be avenged. The monsters that killed him, fed on him, and discarded him like nothing, would die. They would die horribly and for that, he was thrilled.

The two vampires sat in the chairs. An exterior light on the side of the house provided more than enough illumination for him to see, but he wanted more. He wanted to see their faces, cry to them, and tell them why they were dying. But, more importantly, *who* they were dying for.

His vampire hunters stood around their prey. Each of them had guns, but they were aimed at the ground.

John felt like they were on an island. The darkness was surrounding them and their insignificant speck of light. Behind the house was a thick patch of woods. It might as well have been a sheet of black velvet. The gloom was impenetrable. Even with the sky lightening, the woods were dark.

John looked at his watch. The sun would rise soon. The pink sky in the east was getting brighter. Soon, the killing rays would peek out from behind the mountains.

"Take their fucking hoods off. I want to be the last thing they see when they die," John said to no one in particular.

Salim nodded to Arthur. "Take them off. Let's watch these fuckers burn."

The sky turned a shade lighter, cutting through the darkness.

Arthur holstered his gun and stepped behind both of the vampires. He grabbed their hoods and yanked.

John didn't speak, just stared.

The woman, Sarin, was stunning. Her black hair, even though

messy, was glossy. Her skin was flawless and she looked at him like a shark. A slight grin rose on her plump lips, as if she knew something he didn't. John almost flinched from her glare, but he knew it was a ruse. A bluff. The folly of the condemned.

John knew better than to look her in the eyes. He knew a vampire's glamor was just as strong as a snake charmer. He thought his resolve was strong enough to resist, especially knowing what she was, but he wouldn't risk it. Not when he'd come so far.

The boy, Cameron, had his head down. The look of defeat was clear on his face, a youthful face.

John felt pity for him, but only for a second. He knew he wasn't looking at a boy. No, he was gazing upon a killer, an immortal beast that would feast on blood and flesh. Killing indiscriminately as he moved around the country like a fucking plague. He'd even killed a young girl—a child. An innocent girl was used like food and discarded when they'd had their fill.

Well, no more. Parents wouldn't have to cry at night when their children went missing. No wives or husbands wondering if their spouse ran off with a lover. No more trails of mutilated corpses, ripped apart and drained of blood. At least not for these two. Their reign of terror was ending in mere minutes.

"Look at me, boy," John spat. Memories of his son, it was hard even to imagine his name, flashed in his mind. The terror he must've felt at the last moments of his life. The pain of being consumed. John stared at the vampires—he hoped they were fucking scared.

Cameron looked up.

John stood before them, with the vampire hunters flanking each side. He looked over their shoulders to the east, which was even lighter now.

"You don't know me, but I fucking know you. You and your kind took my son from me. Killed him." He paused and cleared his throat. Tears welled in his eyes—tears of anger, joy, and sadness. "Ate him," he yelled and exhaled hard. "Now, now it's your turn to fucking pay. To fucking die!"

Sarin watched the man's performance. His shouts and damnations weren't new to her. But, she knew this was the end and could do without the theatrics.

The other hunters, the three men, and the woman, stood silent. They'd all re-holstered their weapons, knowing the sun was rising. It wouldn't be long.

One of them, Arthur, she believed, stood the closest. He was smirking at her, his eyes glued to her chest.

Untie me and then we'll see if you're still grinning like a fool, she thought. Sarin watched him, trying to get a hold of his eyes. His eyes, firmly affixed to her breasts, weren't moving.

In the gloom of the early morning, Arthur began rubbing himself through his pants. The others couldn't see it, but Sarin could.

The morning was calm, and still. The trees were silent, with not even a gust of wind rattling the leaves.

Yet, Sarin felt something blow by her. Something fast. Something she'd felt before—something from her past.

Arthur's arm, the one he was using to rub his cock, snapped with a loud crack. One moment it had been whole, giving him pleasure; the next, it was mangled, twisted, and spurting blood. He looked at the unnaturally powerful hand gripping his destroyed flesh. The fingers, the cold, undead fingers, ended in claws.

Marcellus, Sarin's creator, ripped Arthur's arm off and bit into his neck.

A fan of blood sprayed from Arthur's destroyed flesh as he flopped to the ground. With his remaining arm, he tried to stem the blood pouring from his torn throat, but he was already dead.

Marcellus looked at the shocked vampire hunters. He opened his arms wide, flexing his clawed fingers. His mouth, his wicked, tooth-filled mouth, split into a carnival-like smile. Rows of sharp teeth glistened in the sensor light. His blonde hair hung shoulder length, framing his chiseled face.

Mary stared at him, captivated by what she was seeing. Marcellus turned his head, his steel-blue eyes catching hers.

His glamor was legendary and it was on full display. There was nothing to see or even let you know he had control of you until it was too late.

Mary cried, her silent tears sliding down her cheeks.

"Fucking kill it," Salim yelled and drew his gun.

Mary had her gun in hand, quicker than Paolo or Salim, but it wasn't aimed at Marcellus; it was aimed at Paolo. Her weapon spat a 9mm bullet into the side of Paolo's head. The crack of the gun—even suppressed—was loud in the still morning, making them flinch. A tangerine-sized hole appeared on the opposite side of his skull, and Paolo fell to the earth, dead.

Salim heard the shot behind him and he snapped his head back, just in time to see Paolo's body hit the earth. The overpressure of the round passing through the man's brain pushed his eyeballs slightly, making them bulge and weep tears of blood.

Mary cried and raised the gun, taking aim at Salim.

"Mary?" he asked, waiting for the bullet to find him.

John rushed forward and grabbed Mary from behind. He wrapped his arms around her, driving the gun's muzzle to the ground. The gun fired, kicking up rocks and dirt. They fought, struggling over the weapon.

Mary cried, trying to free the gun from his grasp…and then she had another urge. She broke three of John's fingers with a snap and wrenched the weapon from his hands. She tried to fight it and knew she was breaking the grasp. But not before the final urge won. The muzzle was still warm as she pressed it underneath her chin. Tears ran down her face as she locked eyes with Salim.

"I love y—," the gun barked, sending the bullet through her soft palate and out of the top of her skull.

Salim watched her fall but knew the threat was in front of him.

Marcellus was done playing with them. The sun was rising, and he knew time was up. He rushed Salim, coming in low.

The vampire hunter raised his gun, aiming. He fired from near point-blank range and missed.

Marcellus had centuries of hunting, centuries of killing, and centuries of being hunted. A gun, especially one he could see, wouldn't be enough. With a twitch of his undead muscles, he dodged the bullets, letting them fly past him with a sizzle.

Salim's eyes went wide and he knew he was dead.

Marcellus tackled him to the ground, landing on his chest. His clawed thumbs darted for Salim's eyes. Sharp, talon-like nails popped the soft eyeballs, seeking the man's brain.

Salim screamed and dropped the gun. He reached up blindly, pulling at Marcellus' arms, which felt like cold steel. The vampire growled in his brutal onslaught.

Ocular jelly and blood oozed from Salim's eye sockets. His scream was silenced when the hellish fingers found his brain. The gray matter yielded beneath the vampire's claws.

Marcellus stood, looking at John. His fingers and mouth dripped gore and he sneered at the old man.

John cradled his broken fingers and looked at the vampire with despair. He was still on the ground and had no desire to stand. He should feel fear, but he only felt failure. Failure to avenge his son. His son, his baby boy, the only love of his life: Nathan.

Marcellus stalked forward, knowing the fight was over. He stood over the wounded man, looking down at him.

"Nathan, I'm sorry," John wept. He looked up at Marcellus with tears in his eyes.

The vampire breathed deeply, taking in his fear and despair. His tongue snaked out, dancing over the serrated rows of teeth.

Marcellus attacked. His hand moved in a blur of death. It struck the side of John's head with a wet smack.

John's jaw dislocated and spun almost under his ear. His flesh tore like old fabric, exposing meat and bone. The strength of the blow partially decapitated him, leaving his neck torn open. A cascade of gore washed over the dirt, which drank the blood greedily.

Marcellus turned and looked to the east—the sun was rising. He moved to Sarin and grabbed her. The silver-braided rope burned him, leaving him with a vibrating feeling, but he didn't care. Carrying her was like lifting a bag of feathers. He rushed towards the house with unnatural speed and grace and smashed into the back door.

The door erupted in a shower of splinters as the vampires entered.

The sun rose.

The screams were horrible; for a moment, Sarin thought Marcellus had been trapped outside. Then she remembered Cameron.

Sarin stood back from the doorway, careful not to let any light touch her, but she had to watch.

"Sarin!" Cameron screamed as the golden rays scorched his undead flesh. "Sarin, please fucking save me!" His skin bubbled and popped, weeping mucousy blood and ichor. "Please!" Cameron thrashed in the chair and fell to the ground. He strained against the rope, which only caused it to bite into the meat of his upper arms. Cameron tried to stand, willing his body to run for safety, but he couldn't.

Cameron's pleas degraded from words, to guttural moans of agony. His flesh sizzled and smoked. Blisters formed and popped like a pot of sauce, ready to boil over. His eyes turned black, drooling pus down his cheeks, finding its way into his open mouth. Cameron's tongue, which had tasted countless drops of blood, split like an overcooked sausage. Gore poured down his throat, smoking with the foul odor of burned, rotten flesh. With the last ounce of strength he had, Cameron tried to roll and escape the sun.

A low moan escaped his charred throat. Cameron's corpse smoked and before Sarin's tear-strewn eyes, burst into flames.

It wasn't a gradual fire; this was a torch turned to the max. Flames shot from his body, hot white, bordering on blue. It was pure immolation. And then, the fire guttered out, leaving behind a pile of ash. The wind, which had been absent the entire morning, made an appearance. It lifted Cameron's still-hot ashes into the air and carried him away. The only thing left behind was a patch of charred earth and a melted chair. And like he'd never even been there, Cameron was gone.

"Are you alright?" Marcellus asked. He pulled Sarin away from the doorway. The sun was still rising, and its dangerous rays crept into the house.

Sarin allowed herself to be guided, leaving the scene of carnage and death behind her. She looked up at her creator, the being who'd saved her as a human, giving her a new life—an undead life. A being who left her, who crushed her, yet again, saved her.

"Marcellus," she said. His name felt foreign on her lips. She said it before, but it felt different with him standing before her. He'd changed back, looking like himself again. His blonde hair was slightly disheveled, with one strand hanging over his nearly black left eye. She reached up and touched the stubble on his chiseled cheeks. This looked like a loving gesture, but it wasn't. It was done out of sheer amazement. To confirm he was there, standing in front of her.

"What, did you think I was going to let them kill you?" he said with a grin. "I've had Salim and his crew on my radar for years. I became suspicious when my contacts told me they were heading to the States. Little did I expect to find them hunting one of my best," he looked her up and down, "creations."

Sarin's black heart quivered. There was plenty of good for all the bad times she spent with him. Her body shuddered as it recalled his touch—the things they'd done to each other, for each other.

Cameron, his name flashed into her mind. Sarin looked back towards the yard full of sunlight and corpses.

"I assume he was yours?" Marcellus asked, his tone dripping with jealousy.

Sarin nodded. "He was only a few years old. He saved me once and I saved him." She sighed.

"Well, he's dead, ashes to ashes, dust to dust. Or whatever that fucking stupid book says." He put his hand out, beckoning her to take it. "Come on, let's see if this place has a basement. I'm exhausted and I have lots to tell you."

Sarin took his hand and let herself be guided deeper into the black house. Her life, once again, had almost ended, only to be ripped from the jaws of death by this man. She'd escaped the insanity Marcellus had brought once. This time, she didn't think she'd be as lucky.

They found the door to the basement and slowly made their way into the cold darkness. A slight breeze worked its way through the house, pushing the door. It swung, crying on unoiled hinges, and slammed shut.

DANIEL J. VOLPE

Daniel J. Volpe is an author of extreme horror and splatterpunk. His love for horror started at a young age when his grandfather unwittingly rented him, A Nightmare on Elm Street. Daniel has published with D&T Publishing, Potters Grove, The Evil Cookie Publishing, and self-published. He can be found on Facebook @ Daniel Volpe, Instagram @ dj_volpe_horror , Twitter @DJVolpeHorror and DanielJVolpeHorror@gmail.com

ABOUT THE EDITOR / PUBLISHER

Dawn Shea is an author and half of the publishing team over at D&T Publishing. She lives with her family in Mississippi. Always an avid horror lover, she has moved forward with her dreams of writing and publishing those things she loves so much.

D&T Previously published material:
ABC's of Terror
After the Kool-Aid is Gone

Follow her author page on Amazon for all publications she is featured in.
Follow D&T Publishing at the following locations:
Website
Facebook: Page / Group
Or email us here: dandtpublishing20@gmail.com

Black Hearts and Red Teeth by Daniel J. Volpe

Edited by Patrick C. Harrison III

Cover by Don Noble

Formatting by J.Z. Foster

Black Hearts and Red Teeth

Made in the USA
Coppell, TX
25 March 2023